Expecting Jesus

Expecting Jesus

Sonya Contreras

Bull Head Press

Scripture taken from the NEW AMERICAN STANDARD BIBLE®, Copyright ©1960, 1962, 1963, 1968, 1971, 1972, 1973, 1975, 1977, 1995 by the Lockman Foundation. Used by permission.

Expecting Jesus is a work of fiction. Although retelling the Scriptures' events as closely as possible, the real people, events, establishments, and locales are used fictitiously. All other elements of the novel are drawn from the author's imagination.

Published by Bull Head Press
Squaw Valley, California
Paperback ISBN-13: 9780999000953
eBook ISBN-10: 0999000950

Library of Congress Control Number: 2017915601
CreateSpace Independent Publishing Platform
North Charleston, South Carolina

Cover Design by Kirk DouPonce of DogEared Design
Copy edited by Titania Porter
Formatting by Joseph Contreras, Jr.
Typeface: Felix Titling, Bell MT, and Constantia

Printed in the United States of America

"And there are also many other things which Jesus did,
which if they were written in detail,
I suppose that even the world itself would not contain the books
that would be written."

John 21:25

Dear Reader,

We all live by what we believe. Our expectations flow from our beliefs. If we believe wrong, our expectations will be wrong.

If we have a wrong view of God, we expect Him to act according to our expectations. We're disappointed when He doesn't do what we think He should. We don't trust Him. Yet we hang onto our beliefs until our dying breath leads us to find truth at last.

These stories reflect the way people see Jesus. All saw Jesus through the lens of what they wanted Him to be. Jesus stripped away their wants until they acknowledged their need. Only then were they able to see Him as He is. Some never saw Him aside from their wants. They clung to their lies and died without hope. Others turned to Him and allowed Him to change them. Instead of seeking their own desires, they found Him.

As you read their stories, may you see people looking to Jesus and learn from what they found. Then search His Word to see Him more. Not as Who we want to see, but as He truly is. Then our expectations will be right, and we will truly know Him.

Sonya Contreras

Who did the Jews expect Jesus to be?

A man who announced His coming, was not a religious leader, but dressed in camel's hide, eating locusts.

The Messiah came.

He was the Long Expected One.

But the people expected someone different.

They expected Him to come in glory; He was placed in a manger by a lowly virgin.

They expected a king; He came as a servant.

They expected Him to overthrow the Romans; He came as an obedient subject.

They expected Him to overthrow Rome; His power could conquer any government.

They expected that money could buy position; He asked for their hearts.

When they saw Him, they expected only the Jews to be helped; He came to help the Samaritan who had faith.

They expected Him to call the mighty, He went to the weak.

They expected Him to condemn the publicans, sinners, and prostitutes; He forgave them and asked them to follow Him.

They expected him to be independent; He relied on His Father.

They expected tolerance for their religious ways; He said, "I am the only way."

They expected to continue in their darkness; He shined His light on all areas.

They hated Him; He loved them.

They perpetuated self-reliance; He relied on His Father.

They gloried in their own self-righteousness; He imparted His perfect righteousness.

They expected to continue in their sin; He rebuked it.

When questioned by the rulers to catch Him in His words, He left them silent.

When beaten, He took it.

When denied, He expected it.

When rejected, He stood alone.

He didn't call twelve legions of angels, but submitted to death.

When Jesus came to the Jews, they weren't ready for Him.

Their expectations didn't match what Jesus did.

Jesus didn't fulfill people's expectations.

His actions surprised them.

His words silenced them.

Who are we expecting?

We weren't expecting the Jesus Who came.

Are you suffering today and demanding that Jesus to take it away?

Are you confused because of what you expected God to do for you?
Are you questioning whether God has the right to do this to you?

What do you expect of Jesus?
Go to the Scriptures and allow Jesus to open your understanding.
He will change your expectations and surpass what you thought.

Contents

I am Simeon

As I was eating the first meal of the day, my family made plans. I wasn't listening. My thoughts were on the Lord—how soon would He call me to Him? My wife had already gone to live with Him. I missed her these three years. I couldn't wait, yet I couldn't leave this life until I saw the Lord's Christ. He had told me that. I must wait. And so I waited. But it was hard.

I chewed another bite of flatbread. I no longer tasted. I was grateful for the few teeth I had. But, oh, I wanted to see the Lord. With the Lord, I would no longer need this old body. Or these few teeth. He would make me whole again—not only in body.

I must go to the Temple today. It was not the Sabbath, nor a feast day. But the Lord had something to tell me.

"Father, would that be pleasing?"

I hadn't even heard my son. "What?"

He repeated his words, slowly, as if I wouldn't understand them. "We need your help at the market today."

I'd forgotten it was market day. I cleared my throat. Now that my hands could no longer form clay around the potter's wheel, I did nothing to support the family. But I could sell the vases and bowls at market. Market day was important. We depended on the sales to pay taxes. I shook my head. "I can't go today."

My son stared, his mouth open, but he didn't speak.

I looked around the table. It had grown quiet. "I'll go to the Temple today."

My daughter-in-law patted my hand. "It's not the Sabbath yet, Father."

I felt my son's scrutiny, like I wasn't just losing my physical capacities, but now was losing my mind. I nodded. "The Lord wants me at the Temple today."

My son stared out the door, biting his lip. He had been deciding the family's activites, consulting me only as a token of respect. He expected me to sell our things at the marketplace. He licked his lips, finally nodding. "I'll prepare the donkey for you."

I wouldn't put my family in any worse position than I had already by not going to market. I raised my hand. "You'll need the donkey with the cart for market. I'll walk."

My son's wife reminded me, "Can you climb the stairs on your own?"

I'd find a way to climb the Temple stairs. This inner prompting wasn't my own whims. I must obey. "I'll be fine."

I set off for the Temple after the meal. The Lord had something to show me. Excitement bubbled within me.

My legs weren't strong. I leaned against houses lining the streets to keep from stumbling.

Jerusalem's streets were already crowded. Merchants displayed their wares outside the Temple steps for those travelers who couldn't bring their animals for sacrifice.

I didn't feel the urgency to get to the Temple anymore. Had I heard wrong? Should I have gone to the market for my son?

While I paused, I noticed a couple.

The man sheltered a woman with child. They studied the lambs for sale. That would be for their sin offering. He asked the price, shook his head, and moved up the street where pigeons and turtledoves were sold. They examined each cage. He pointed to a pair at the end, tucked away from view.

The merchant, at first, wouldn't acknowledge him. This wasn't one of his high-paying clients. When he finally gave a price, the man shook his head. They haggled a few minutes, but the merchant wouldn't lower his price. The man counted out his last coin. "We must have two."

The merchant shook his head, turning away to help a wealthy buyer.

The couple waited for the bird they had purchased.

The woman swayed from side to side, cooing to the baby. "We can only give what we have."

The man was frustrated. "But the sacrifice demands two birds. That is the very least we are to give."

I stepped forward and waved to the merchant. "How much for that pigeon?" I knew what my son would say, "Father, you can't give to every poor beggar on the street." But this man hadn't begged. He walked like a man only recently fallen on rough times, and weary at that.

I paid for the pigeon, nodding to the couple's cage. "Put it with theirs."

When the birds were settled in the cage, the man embraced me. "May God bless you."

I patted him on the back. "He does. Shalom."

The woman's eyes filled with tears. "Be at peace."

I rested my hand on the child's head. "May the Lord's salvation come soon."

I turned now to the Temple. I paused before the Temple stairs. On the Sabbath, I leaned heavily on my son to climb each step. How would I make them now? I looked to the top in despair. The prompting in my heart increased. I must go up them.

Behind me, someone gently held the crook of my arm. "May I help?"

I looked into the face of the man who bought the pigeon.

I smiled. "That you may."

I leaned heavily on him as he half-carried me up the stairs.

The man was strong; he held me secure with gentleness. Even as he supported me, he carried the pigeon cage. His wife and child stayed by his side.

Reaching the top of the stairs, the man helped me to a column. "You are fine?"

I leaned against the column, catching my breath. I nodded.

"Wait for me. I'll help you down the stairs when we're finished."

I nodded. The Lord's peace rested on me. The words that I had spoken to the child played in my mind as I watched them present their sacrifice to the priest for their burnt and sin offering. "May the Lord's salvation come soon."

The Lord's Spirit came upon me.

I knew why I was here. I followed them. I grabbed the man's elbow, just as he had taken hold of mine at the stairs.

He turned. "You are well?"

I motioned to hold the baby.

The woman hesitated, but handed him to me.

I squeezed him against my chest. I could barely speak as God's Spirit told me why I had come to the Temple. "Lord, You may take Your servant." I paused to swallow, the tears pooling in my eyes. "For my eyes have seen Your salvation given to all people, a light to the Gentiles, and the glory of Your people Israel."

The baby wiggled.

I feared to hold Him longer, lest I drop Him. I regretfully handed Him back to his mother. Hesitant to leave him, I rested my hand on his head. The woman looked at me. I smiled, though the words were hard. "A sword will pierce your soul."

Her eyes widened and she bent her head down.

The Lord had heard the cries of His people and sent His salvation!

I stood straighter, taller. The Lord had heard our prayers. My heart sang. My insides bubbled with excitement. We would wait no more for His salvation.

The man, true to his offer, helped me down the stairs. He offered to walk me home.

I shook my head. I couldn't stop smiling. I didn't feel my aching, crippled hands. I wouldn't stumble over my awkward feet.

I could have danced home! My joy was complete. My peace was full.

I arrived home, telling my family of the One I had met.

They were appeasing, skeptical.

I went to sleep, knowing when I awoke, I'd be with Him Who had come to save His people. I could die in peace. I had seen the Lord's Anointed.

Salvation had come to our people.

The Lord had done what He said He would do.

I am Herod the Great

I RULED JUDEA FOR Rome. Within a year of my appointment, civil war broke out. I escaped to Rome, where the emperor granted me the title "King of Judea" and gave me an army. I proved worthy by quenching revolts. I kept order with secret police, informing of betrayers. Two thousand soldiers, chosen from distinguished veterans and young men from influential Jewish families became my bodyguards.

I not only guarded my throne from outside sources, but also from within. I banished one wife and her child when I married my teenage niece to gain Jewish favor and secure my kingdom. I appointed my 17-year-old brother-in-law as high priest, fearing he would otherwise dethrone me. Then one year later, during a party, I commanded his drowning. I executed one wife on adultery charges imagined by my sister. I executed two sons for high treason and eliminated any family members who didn't please me.

My throne was established.

I then made Israel into the commerce and trade center.

I became the "greatest builder in Jewish history." I built aqueducts, theatres, and grand temples for the gods. I restored the Jewish Temple, which I called "Herod's Temple." I even created new cities as part of my legacy and was proclaimed "President of the Olympics" for life after donating money for their continuation.

Of course, building came at great cost, and so I taxed the people of Judea heavily.

Leaders cried against supporting my lavish spending, elaborate entertainment, and expensive gifts. They didn't understand my need to ensure my position.

Although raised a Jew, I wasn't accepted by the religious leaders. They didn't approve of my decadent lifestyle. Nor did they like the golden eagle I put at my Temple's entrance. They cried against it as idolatry. They claimed I ignored their demands. They weren't consoled when I relieved their Sadducees, replacing them with high priests from Babylonia and Alexandria. They stirred up their people against Roman rule, creating unrest.

Jews are so hard to please.

They would never understand that I couldn't obey their strict laws and still keep my throne.

They did see the better waterways I built for Jerusalem, and the grander temples for their worship. Construction brought jobs. It kept the people busy, so they wouldn't have time for revolts.

I was lying on my couch, wondering what other constructions I could add to my legacy, when a messenger entered.

He bowed to the ground seven times at my feet. "Men, astrologers from the East, seek your wise counsel."

I drank from my vessel. No one sought my counsel, unless they wanted my throne. I studied their caravan from my window. They were men of great wealth. It would be wise to see what they wanted.

"I'll see them in my throne room."

Checking my robe for crumbs and putting on my crown, I allowed them entrance.

They bowed, presenting me with presents. Their caravan outside my window promised more than just these tokens.

I licked my lips. Did they wait for my wisdom before they gave me more?

"Where is He Who is born King of the Jews?"

They asked as if I should be expecting this king.

I paced. They questioned my right as king? *I* was the only king appointed for the Jews.

"We saw His star and came to worship Him."

I paused my pacing. A star? I shut my mouth before I could issue threats. I felt my face flush, as I attempted to hide my anger. Another king, while I am on my throne? "I will find this King Who demands that a star shine for Him." I sneered, needing to stay in control.

The chief of their men nodded. "Don't you have counselors who know where the Child is born?"

I dared not look ignorant before them. "Go and refresh yourselves." I dismissed them with a wave of my hand. "We will talk later."

When they left, I turned on the leader of my body guards, demanding, "Why haven't I been told of this King?"

The chief guard bowed low. "No one threatens your throne. Your throne is secure."

I waved my arms. "Men from other countries know of this King. And you know nothing?"

My advisor stepped forward and spoke in a soothing voice, "Perhaps by consulting the Jews' chief scribes, they may know of the One these men seek."

I summoned the Jewish scribes.

They all clustered together, as ignorant as I over this King that was to come, until one stepped forward hesitantly. "Our prophet Micah foretold, *'Out of Bethlehem a ruler shall come who will shepherd My people Israel.'*"

"Bethlehem?" I bellowed. "What king would come from a town so small?"

My advisor leaned toward me. "Tell the men to look in Bethlehem. If they find Him, have them return to tell you."

I rubbed my hands together. The plan would work. I called for the wise men.

I questioned what they knew. I walked them to the door. "Find the Child. Report to me, so I, too, may worship Him."

The men agreed and left.

I planned. I worshiped no one but me. I could allow no one on my throne.

I waited. I paced.

After three weeks, I confronted my advisor. "Why haven't they returned?"

The advisor fidgeted a distance from me. "Maybe if you sent a messenger to find the wise me . . ."

My face grew hot. My head throbbed. "I should've sent my army with them to ensure their return. Why didn't you suggest that to me?"

I stalked to the window and glanced out. When I saw my body guards outside the palace doors, I knew what I would do. I glanced at my advisor.

He turned pale.

I laughed. "No King can dethrone me. Bring in my General of the Army."

The advisor scurried to leave.

When my general entered, I was calm. I tapped my fingers on the window sill. This would take care of the problem. "Take my army to Bethlehem and the surrounding area." I gained momentum as I explained my plan. "Kill all the male children two years and under."

The General fingered his sword and nodded. He backed from the room before I could think of anything else. I heard him walking down the corridor.

I clasped my hands in satisfaction. Then I lost my smile. "General!"

He returned. "Yes, Sire?"

"Prepare my chariot. I'll go and ensure this deed is done."

He nodded. "As you wish, Sire."

I stormed Bethlehem with my army. I would remove this King.

The army barged into every house and every room for every child.

Women begged for mercy.

I had no mercy for kings that would dethrone me, even a star-bearing King.

None were left alive.

No wise men from the East would deceive me and keep their secret.

I laughed. I had won.

When I returned home, I took to my bed, not feeling well. My chest tightened. My breathing came in gasps. My body wouldn't cooperate with what my mind told it to do. I shook and convulsed against my will.

I became a prisoner in my own bed, tormented by extreme pain, unable to even take my own life.

I planned my funeral. My death must be mourned. I would guarantee it.

I decreed that a group of distinguished men should be killed at my death. Thus, my death would be grieved by many. The grief I craved would be insured.

Herod, the Great, died . . . lonely . . . out of favor with Rome . . . without being mourned by any, in spite of his elaborate plans.

He did not worship the true King of the Jews.

He didn't even know his plot to kill Him had failed.

But he did finally acknowledge the One Who could have saved him.

I am Salazar, Chief of the Persian Wisemen

WE MAGI HAVE been trained in science, agriculture, mathematics, history and astrology to serve the Persian kings ever since the days when Daniel was the chief of the magi for many years. Many of his Jewish practices were adopted, because of their truth. His God explained dreams that no others could.

Daniel prophesied of a world-ruler coming after seventy weeks. He would restore and rebuild Jerusalem. The entire world waits for this Jewish king to arrive. We watch for it. We expect it.

The time has come.

Those were my thoughts as Kadir, the expert magus in astronomy, waited for my attention. His eyes glowed with excitement.

"What is it?"

"Come see."

I followed him to the roof of the palace. I knew it was important by the bounce in his step. My heart beat faster. Was it the Coming One?

Kadir pointed. "It's so simple. This God of the Jews leads His people clearly. Their prophecy is fulfilled. Look!"

The sky was clear. The stars shone brightly. And a new star was shining more brightly than all the others.

I gasped. "It's brighter than the Morning Star!"

Kadir pointed over my shoulder. "Notice what constellation it's in."

"The constellation Virgo, the virgin who has a child; and the star points to Coma, the constellation of the child. Coma means 'desired one' or 'longed for one.' He is longed for."

Kadir smiled. "Yes, And the new star completes the Coma, the constellation of the child from the virgin. The Christ-Child is here, born of a virgin. What will we do?"

I couldn't take my eyes from the sight. The story was in the sky, as if I was reading it from a scroll in my hand. "We must go and see this King."

Seeing the star created a stir in the palace.

I decided who would go. Some were merely curious adventurers, wanting to see what a Child-King that would rule the world looked like. But others had watched longingly for the signs, and had listened not just with their ears but with their hearts. Those men would go. I chose twelve men to journey with me to Judea.

Kadir bowed before me in my chamber. "I have a request."

I was surprised. Kadir didn't seek people out to make requests. He lived with his studies and included people only when he must.

I was busy with preparations. What gifts should we bring? What would be worthy of such a King? I didn't have time for interruptions. "What is it?"

Kadir cleared his throat. "I wish to go with you."

I laughed.

His face fell. He misread my laughter.

I grabbed his shoulder. "You're the first I had chosen to go."

He sighed, like a weight had been lifted. "Thank you. I must see this King Who holds all the earth's deliverance in His hands. I must know Him. My heart is empty. This King alone can fill me."

Kadir wasn't one to speak much. I knew this message came from his heart.

This is what I sought, too. I nodded. "We'll find Him together."

Kadir bounced on his toes, a sign he needed to return to his studies away from people.

I squeezed his shoulder. "You will go. And will stay by me."

I laughed at his eyes' bigness. The caravan was arranged by order of importance. Those most important were protected by those who went before and after. I was the chief of the magi and held the place of honor. Many assumed that the next magus, who was being trained to take my place, would sit beside me. He was not going. Kadir would sit beside me. "This King will do more for the world than any king that has come before or after Him. We must prepare."

He bounced out of the room. I knew the honor I bestowed on him did not make him bounce, but the prospect of meeting this King did.

I felt the same way. When I turned back to my packing, I realized all my anxiety had left me. Only my need to know this King remained.

Our caravan required an army escort. The king provided well for us, his counsellors, because we reflected his power and his throne. Robbers were sure to be attracted to our rich robes and kingly attire and would be tempted by the gifts we carried to the new King.

We had traveled many days before reaching the city of Jerusalem. Slowing our camels, we advanced through the crowded streets.

When we arrived at the palace, we were amazed at the splendor. King Herod had been busy during his many years as king. What kind of palace would he construct for the new King?

We were ushered into his presence and bowed before him.

Herod didn't even lift his head to acknowledge us. In Persia, we were use to being treated with honor by our own king. He depended upon our counsel for his kingdom, safety, and life. Herod's reception made me doubt him, even as I asked, "Where is He Who is born King of the Jews?"

Herod, visibly shaken by the news, leaped up and began pacing. His face flushed. I could see his heart, pounding through all his layers of clothing.

Herod was a Jew. Didn't he know their own prophecies of the Coming One? Weren't they looking for their own King? I couldn't fathom such ignorance, nor excuse his lack of preparation.

I rose to my feet. "Daniel, the Magus of your people, prophesied of a Coming One who would deliver His people. The 490 years he spoke of is completed."

Kadir could not contain his excitement. "The Child is here."

"Child?" Herod spoke like an ignorant man.

Must we tell him all the prophecies of his own coming King? We only knew what Daniel had told us. Their other prophets should have told them more. "The King will save His people."

Herod clutched at the arm of his throne and sat again, as if the information taxed him.

No one stepped forward to advise him. "Don't you have counselors who could find where the Child is born?"

Herod stared ahead. "Why haven't I been told about Him?"

I shook my head. Even the Romans knew this King would come out of Judea. That's why one of their emperor's wanted Jerusalem to be his capital rather than Rome.

I tried to contain my disgust. This is what comes when rulers are appointed to thrones, rather than being born to them. They aren't trained, yet they rule a people? I calmed my irritation. I must find the King, even if His own people weren't looking for Him. "The whole world waits His coming."

Herod pulled his beard. His brow furrowed. "I must consult with my chief priests and scribes. I will let you know."

I didn't trust him. Yet we had no other option. I nodded as we turned to go.

Later, in a private consultation with us, Herod appeared much calmer.

One of his scribes read from his scrolls "Out of Bethlehem a Ruler shall come Who will shepherd My people Israel."

He asked what we knew.

Kadir shared eagerly of what he had seen. In his child-like innocence, he thought all desired to know the King as he did. "According to when I first saw the star, the Child could be almost two years old."

I cringed. I didn't want this ruler to know any more about the King. I didn't trust him. But I needed his help to find Him. He had the Law of the Jews.

"In Bethlehem." That was all they knew? We had come this far. We would go and see. Someone there should be able to point us to the King.

As we turned to go, Herod followed us to the door of his chamber. "Find the Child. Then report to me, so that I, too, may worship Him."

I didn't consent. I didn't trust him.

The guard at the gate of Bethlehem questioned us, "What business do you have?"

We told of our search. "Where is He who is born King of the Jews?"

He looked confused. "You mean, King Herod?"

Were these people so ignorant? I shook my head, biting my tongue. I ached to see the King. The pressure in my heart had increased as we traveled. We were so close.

This people weren't looking for their King. They knew nothing. They cared nothing.

Kadir asked me, "How will we find Him?"

I shook my head. "We'll camp outside the walls of the city tonight. I'll know what to do in the morning."

He nodded.

I swallowed. I didn't know what another night camping in the desert would bring. I wished the stars would answer. Why had I given Kadir confidence?

His eyes reflected his heart's need. It mirrored my own heart. We longed for wholeness.

I had wisdom, wealth, power; but my heart yearned for something more. I felt, like Kadir, that this King would have the answer. If this God had brought us this far, then He could direct us to His King.

That night, after all had gone to sleep, except the guards of our army escort, I lingered over my vessel of warmed camel milk. I thought about this King.

I must have dozed, for I dreamed of Herod. We shouldn't return to Herod. He shouldn't know where the Child is. My dream assured me we would find the Child. I woke with peace.

In the morning, Kadir dressed in his finest and sat on his camel. If one could bounce on a camel, he would have, waiting for my signal to begin. He met my eye.

I laughed. "Yes, Kadir. We will meet Him today."

We entered the city. The other magi followed me; an unusual request, but I must lead them to the King. This God would show me. We left the main streets of Bethlehem, turning down side streets. Our caravan went single file on nothing but rutted pathways.

How could anyone live in such poverty? We would find the King here? Had I taken a wrong turn? But I pushed onward, compelled by a sense of direction, I pushed onward.

People watched us from doorways and windows.

I felt the need to stop. I dismounted. I bowed to a man who stood at his doorway "Where is He who is born King of the Jews?"

He smiled and motioned us inside. Had he expected us? We left our soldiers to guard the caravan. As all twelve of us crowded into his humble house.

Where were the other worshipers of this new King?

Once my eyes adjusted to the dark interior, I saw a young mother holding a Child. He was the King Whom we sought. I fell to my knees on that dirt floor, bowed my head and cried. "We have found the King!"

I could not rise for a long time. My heart was full.

This Babe would bring deliverance.

"Tell us about the Child." It was Kadir.

We listened as the mother and man told of the angel's visits. How the woman, as virgin, had conceived by the Holy Spirit and borne a Child. How the angels had told shepherds.

I looked around the house. They were lowly people, of lowly birth. The man's hands were hands of a tradesman, a carpenter. "Why are you here?" I asked. My question confused them. "Shouldn't a king be treated like a king?"

The man smiled sadly. "Our people don't believe."

I nodded, understanding dawning. "A woman not married, a true virgin, but not believed."

The man looked me in the eye, relieved that I had put it into words. Nothing more was said.

That night, Kadir showed the man the star.

The man stood straighter. He embraced Kadir. "I'll look at the star and be reassured when the people do not believe and times are hard. Thank you."

I watched the embrace: this humble man, with his shabby cloak full of patches, against Kadir's silk cloak of sapphire blue. The men were the same. Kadir believed. This man, Joseph, believed. The King was uniting people of every class to know Him, even before He could talk.

We lingered over our worship, over our meal, over our visit. I didn't want to leave. But I felt an urging, a sense that the longer we stayed, the more danger we brought to the Child. I remembered my dream of Herod. We must leave.

Before we left, we gave the Child gold, frankincense, and myrrh. I looked at the gifts laid out before him. They were gifts commonly given to any king. But this time, they didn't seem enough.

The man, Joseph, walked us to his door. He hesitantly put his hand on my shoulder, perhaps feeling his lowly class, but emotional from the gift. "I can't thank you enough for the gifts." He swallowed. "I would work for Him, but no one will pay for my services. They only see the Child, born without a father." He paused and looked down. When he raised his eyes to meet mine, they held tears. "Our needs have been great. Your gifts will help. Thank you."

I felt ashamed at my meager offering. I had thought it great when preparing to leave my country. In this house, so needy and lowly, I felt I should have given all that I owned, and yet it still would not have been enough.

I longed to stay with this Infant. To see how He would grow and deliver His people and the world. I looked one more time at the mother with the Child. Then I tore my gaze away and walked quickly to our awaiting camels.

I had met the King and worshipped. The longing in my heart was satisfied. This Child would deliver His people. He would deliver us all. I could not wait.

We journeyed back to our country a different way to avoid Herod. We didn't want to risk bringing danger to the Child.

We had been traveling many hours when I asked Kadir, "What do you think?"

Kadir looked over the hills of Israel toward the east and home. "This Hebrew God unites people from all over the world, from every class and people, not by force or power or military might, but by reaching into their hearts and pulling them to His own heart. But not everyone will know Him. He won't coerce them; He petitions, like a servant, allowing them to choose. Yet someday, He will demand that all acknowledge Him as King, not just of the Jews, but of all people, of all time."

Again, Kadir surprised me with his wisdom and the expression of his heart. He expressed my own thoughts. I looked at the sky, even though the stars didn't shine in the daylight.

We had found the King.

We had worshipped.

Now what should we do?

Kadir was not finished. "I'll wait until the King delivers my heart from its bondage. Then I'll be truly free."

I would wait, too. The people had waited 490 years for His birth. It was a small thing to wait for His deliverance. But my heart didn't want to wait too long. I longed to know Him now.

I am James

IAM THE SECOND son of Mary.

My father, Joseph, tried to raise me to love wood. He could look at a piece of wood and feel its value, strength, gift. I would nod, but couldn't see as he did.. Wood made us money. I saw no other value.

Jesus tried to convince me to see wood differently. "See this tree. Don't you wonder why it leans so far to the left?"

I would look, but only so He would stop asking, and I'd shrug. "Must have been some wind storm."

He would rub his hand over the bark. "But it stood the winds, didn't it, James? It held strong and didn't fall." He studied me with those piercing eyes, like He was telling me a deeper message.

I turned away. I didn't like to be reminded that I couldn't make decisions. I must know all the options before I did anything. That kept me from acting. I frustrated Dad. He would say, "Don't just stare at it! Take the piece of wood and do something with it."

My brother Jude laughed. "Just sell the wood like that, James. By the time you figure out what to make from it, you'll be dead anyway."

Jude could jump into things recklessly—and still be safe. I must know I was safe before I got there.

And Jesus . . . he always pricked my heart. He was so good. When we boys would get into mischief, He hindered any fun. He was like my second conscience! Only it was worse than the one inside my head, because it would never let me do anything wrong. He always did what was true. He was so convicting.

Do you know what it's like to follow in the footsteps of a perfect son?

I hated Him!

When Jesus was twelve, my parents couldn't find him after we had traveled a whole day's journey from Jerusalem, where we had kept the Passover. We left the caravan's safety and returned to the Temple. We searched everywhere for him.

Mom was frantic.

I was secretly pleased.

Jesus was finally in trouble.

I couldn't wait for Him to be punished.

When we found Him, He was sitting with the Temple teachers. They were questioning Him about what He understood about the Law.

Mom asked, "Son, why have you treated us so?"

"Don't you know I must be about My Father's business?"

I looked at Dad. This had nothing to do with being a carpenter. What was Jesus talking about?

Dad rested his hand on Jesus's shoulder and squeezed.

Why didn't Dad reprove Jesus? And what business of His Father's was he referring to? That was my first inkling that truth was withheld from me.

I remember in synagogue class, the boy behind me, Simon, whispered, "Your mother's a —."

I turned to face him. He couldn't be calling my mother *that*. "What?"

Just then the Rabbi hit me on the head with his stick.

I looked up startled, turned around in my seat, and bent over my scroll again. But Simon's words stayed in my head all morning. When class was over, I waited for him outside the synagogue. I would defend my mother's honor. My voice shook, "What did you call my mother?"

He repeated the name.

I didn't hesitate. I punched him in his fat, pudgy gut.

He grunted, hunching over. But when he stood again, he lunged at me, swinging.

I was ready. I had never fought before, but I would fight for my mom.

I don't remember the punches. I only remembered the name. No one would defile my mother's character.

The Rabbi separated us, rebuked me, and sent me home.

I walked home, battered and beaten, but the battle wasn't over.

As I kicked a stone down the lane towards home, I wondered how I would explain this to my dad.

Dad met me before I reached his carpenter's shop. He must have been watching for me, wondering why I had taken so long to return home. He didn't say a word, just laid his hand on my shoulder and squeezed.

I hadn't cried when I was fighting. I hadn't cried when the Rabbi rebuked me. But now I could feel tears filling my eyes and running down my face.

My dad bent in front of me and put both hands on my shoulders.

It was then that I felt the pain from the dishonor, from the words that were said. I couldn't look into his eyes. I bowed my head and sobbed.

He grabbed me and crushed me against his chest. He didn't speak. He only held me.

When I had finished crying, he held me at arms' length. "Did they call your mother a name?"

My surprise couldn't have been greater. "How'd you know?"

My dad smiled, a sad, knowing smile. "They can't believe."

I didn't understand his answer. I wanted to ask, "Who? Believe what?" But the pain in my father's eyes kept me from speaking.

My father nodded. "You did what was right. You stood for truth. Your mother didn't sin. But . . ."

My head fell to my chest. Dad wouldn't tell me I shouldn't fight for my mother's honor, would he?

My father waited until I looked him in the face again. "They don't believe the truth. You must know the truth and fight for it. But sometimes fighting means waiting and letting God show them."

"How do I know when to wait and when to fight?"

Father squeezed my shoulders and sighed. "Know the truth first. Then God will show you."

My father spoke in riddles. What truth?

My father stood and walked to his workshop.

I walked beside him. What did he mean?

When we reached his workshop, he pointed to the house. "Have your mother see to your eye. You'll have a black one for sure. But I'm glad you're willing to fight." He tapped my shoulder before entering his shop.

I walked slowly to the house. I didn't relish what my mom would say.

I stood in the doorway for a time, letting my eyes adjust to the dark interior.

When my mother saw me, she hurried over, wrapping her comforting arms around me. "Oh, my son . . ." She shook her head and treated my wounds.

Now I could feel them. My pounding head told me I would feel them for a long time. I closed my eyes tightly, feeling my tears pool as I tried to keep them from falling.

When she had finished, she sat beside me and put her hand on my knee, the only place that didn't throb.

She didn't reprimand. She seemed to know why I had fought, which made me confused. Was it true? The question entered, but I pushed it out as soon as it came.

She just said, "They don't believe."

That's what Father had said. Who? Believe what? I wanted to ask, but couldn't. How would I know the truth?

When my brothers came home from the workshop, Jude admired my puffy face. "James, what a shiner!"

Joseph nodded, knowingly. "Who'd you fight?"

The razzing continued through dinner. But the truth stayed hidden.

Days later when Joseph and I were cleaning out the stable, Joseph said, "About that fight . . ."

I stopped mid-stride, with a shovel full of droppings. "Yeah?"

"What Simon said was true."

I couldn't believe my own brother would admit our mother was capable of such a sin. I dropped my shovel's load. "What?"

Joseph nodded. "I heard family talk. Mom was with child before Dad married her." He paused, "But it's not what you think. I asked Aunt Elizabeth—"

I heard no more. I threw the shovel at his feet and ran beyond the village to the hills. Leaning against a boulder, I hung my head between my knees, gasping for breath.

Over the few days since the fight, I'd had time to consider my parents' words. Doubts had filled my head and clouded my heart.

Comments at family reunions came back to me. I dhadn't understood then, but now they made sense. Jabs at Father; slams at Mother. And my father would just stand, clenching his hands into fists. He worked the muscles of his jaw, a sure sign that he was holding his temper. But he never defended Mom.

So it *was* true!

I saw Jesus in a different way. He divided my folks and the rest of the family. By His goodness, He showed the sin of His parents even more.

I hated Him!

Years later, all of our family stood around my father's bed. Fever had destroyed his body, leaving it wasted. His grip, so strong and true on a piece of wood, was weak as he held my hand.

I was so lost in my thoughts, I almost didn't hear him.

"The angel of the Lord came to me." He paused and swallowed.

I gave him a drink from the dipper beside his bed.

He settled against his cushion. "The angel told me of a Child given to us by the Holy Spirit. We would have a Son, Who would save our people. I was not to touch your mother before He was delivered. The Son would be God-man." The words taxed him.

I squeezed his shoulder, much like he did for me when I needed reassurance. "Rest, Father."

He shook his head. "The words of the angel came true. Mary, your mother, was with child, not by me nor any other man. We were cast out by family and community. No one believed."

He looked at Jesus and nodded. "When it came time for Your birth, we went to Bethlehem to be taxed. No family allowed us to travel with them. We went alone. We had little money, for no one would give me work. Mary was in pain. I remember my helplessness. We stopped many times along the way. Travelers passed us, but we moved too slowly for any to join us.

"When we arrived, the city was crowded. Everything was expensive. We ended up sleeping on the floor of a family who knew Zacharias. Their livestock lived beneath them, as was the custom. They could only give us floor space.

"That night Jesus was born." Dad smiled and touched Jesus's hand. "We put you in a feed box for the animals."

Mom laid her hand on Dad's shoulder and continued the story. "Jesus was born. Shepherds came. Angels told them to follow the star to where the Child was born."

"The shepherds gave us several lambs. We were grateful. Our resources were low. This gift was enough to pay the taxes and start again.

"Even when we went to the Temple, I could give only a poor man's sacrifice for His birth. What a poor provider I was."

Mary shook her head. "Simeon was glad to pay for the second dove."

Dad continued the story, "One day, a caravan came through the dirty streets of the city. I watched from my doorway, wondering if they were lost. No one of such wealth came down our street. They stopped at our door. Imagine my surprise, when they bowed before me on the dirty streets of Bethlehem and asked to see the King. They knelt on the dirt floor and praised God for bringing salvation to the world." Dad rested his head on the cushions for a time before he could continue. "They gave gifts: gold, frankincense, and myrrh. God provided for His Son.

"You can guess the neighbors' and family's response! They watched from their doorways and windows. When our guests left, they were at our doorstep asking for what had been brought!

"That night in a dream, God told me to flee to Egypt to protect His Child. We left during the night, not even telling family. They wouldn't understand. The gifts from the wise men provided for us as we traveled and lived in Egypt.

"After we left, Herod commanded all the children two years and younger to be killed. God protected His Son. Our family and friends' children were not spared.

"When another dream told me it was safe to return, we moved to Nazareth.

"News followed us. Whispers and rumors told of our past. Family resented that we had escaped Herod's massacre. People don't forgive very well. They hold grievances. They believe untruths .... They caused you harm." He paused, looking at all us boys. His eyes rested on Mom. His voice broke, "I couldn't protect you."

I offered him a drink.

He took a sip, and rested.

He had told me to wait for the truth. This was the truth.

But I couldn't accept it. I wouldn't believe.

My father continued. "They would not believe. You boys weren't old enough to understand. We waited to share the truth until you could understand. We wanted Jesus to grow like a normal child. How can anyone understand that God became man and lives with us?" He closed his eyes.

His words from long ago came to my mind. "Know the truth and fight for it. Know when to wait and when to fight." I wasn't ready for the truth. I didn't want to believe. It was easier to believe the untruth.

My father hugged each one of us. He whispered to me, "Know the truth. Fight for it."

I nodded, but didn't want to accept it. If I accepted the truth, I would have to rid my heart of my anger at Jesus.

My dad died that night. But the truth of his words burned into my heart, making me miserable. I fought the truth, and I fought Jesus.

Jesus worked in the workshop day after day with me. I don't know how He could stand me. I wasn't nice. Some days I couldn't even stay. I'd throw down the wood and stomp out of the shop. Conviction was strong on my heart, reminding me of the truth.

When Jesus turned thirty, He approached my mother. "I must be about My Father's business."
My mother nodded, tears forming in her eyes. She hugged him tightly and watched him leave.
I watched him leave, but I held no tears in my eyes.

A distant cousin was getting married. We went to celebrate. We feasted well the first day, but as the day waned, the wine ran out. Mom whispered to Jesus, "They have no more wine."

Jesus said, "My hour has not yet come."

I thought of Dad's words. Sometimes you fight, sometimes you wait. Guess Jesus must wait too. It gave me satisfaction, even though I didn't understand His words.

Mom slipped away and spoke to the servants. She pointed to Jesus.

I thought nothing about it until Jesus spoke to them.

They filled waterpots from the well, drew a pitcher of it and took it to the headwaiter.

I later drank of the water turned to wine. It was good. No, very good. I knew what had happened. But my heart didn't want to believe.

Jesus once spoke in the synagogue in Nazareth. "No prophet is welcome in his hometown. I tell you the truth, in Elijah's day, many widows in Israel went without, during a great famine. Yet Elijah wasn't sent to any of them, but to a widow in Sidon. In Elisha's time, many Hebrew lepers weren't healed, but Naaman, the Syrian, was."

He spoke against me. I was a Jew not accepting His works.

I clenched my fists. I didn't welcome His truth.

The synagogue's religious leaders were also angry. They drove Him from the city, pushing Him toward a cliff to His death. I was with them. I wanted to be the one who pushed Him.

He escaped.

I don't know how.

I kept my distance from Jesus. I disdained His truth that pierced me. I resented His freedom to do what He wanted.

I didn't love wood like my Dad had. I wasn't a good carpenter, no matter how hard I tried.

Joseph had been like Dad, loving the wood into something useful, but he had died, shortly after Dad did.

I supported Mom.

I had married by this time, and I had a family of my own. I moved from my boyhood home, escaping the gossip. We lived in Jerusalem where no one knew me. I could work without being reminded about my family's reputation. But my hatred for Jesus and truth followed me. I wanted nothing to do with Him.

I thrived on the synagogue's rules and regulations. I could measure my goodness against them and not against the goodness of Jesus.

I saw Jesus one more time before His death. He was walking the beach of Galilee by Himself; a rare thing. We nodded to each other.

He hugged and kissed me.

I stood stiff, unyielding to His touch. "You are here for the Feast of Booths?"

He nodded.

Mom wanted me to make sure He came home. "Come to Judea where Your disciples may see Your works. Show Yourself to the world."

I knew the Jewish leaders still weren't pleased with him in Judea. Hadn't they tried to kill Him? I didn't care.

He squeezed my shoulder, as Dad would have done. "My time is not yet here. But this is your time, James. You don't need to wait anymore."

Even as He encouraged me to believe, I shrank from His touch and spewed my hatred. "I am hated by all, because of you."

He shook his head. "The world doesn't hate you, but it hates Me because I show them truth, and their deeds are evil. Go to the feast. I won't go now. My time hasn't come."

I left him then. Even if He said the world hated only Him, I knew my poor treatment was because of Him.

I saw Him the day He hung on the cross. I went only to get Mother and take her home.

She wouldn't leave Him.

I looked at Him. My brother's face was unrecognizable. It was streaked with blood from a crown of three-inch thorns pushed into His head. His beard was ripped off. Blood dripped from His chin. He was stripped of his clothes, except a loincloth. He held himself away from the cross. I didn't know why until I saw His back—what was left of it. The beating they gave Him left no flesh.

Each breath pained Him. He lifted his body against the nails of his hands to raise himself up. He grabbed a breath, then fell against the weight of the nails in his feet.

I took a deep breath, as if I, too, couldn't breathe. I turned away, sickened. "Let's go, Mom. I'll take you home."

She shook her head, her face streaked with tears. She knelt where she was.

I couldn't persuade her.

John, one of Jesus's disciples, said, "I'll stay with her."

I nodded, relieved that I'd done what I could. I left.

I returned to my workshop, picking up a piece of wood to work. I couldn't concentrate. My father's words rang in my mind. "They didn't believe." I could still see his sadness, his pain.

I dropped the wood I was attempting to carve. It clattered to the dirt floor. I couldn't find it. It had grown strangely dark.

It was noon, but no light came through the workshop window. I stumbled to the doorway, kicking wood as I went.

The sky was black as night. Suddenly, a storm poured out its vengeance. The heavens seemed to cry.

In the darkness, my father's words pierced me, "You did what was right. You stood for truth."

My father had been proud when I had fought for my mother's honor, even though he couldn't explain the truth at the time.

My father fought his battle silently, waiting, because they wouldn't believe.

My father would have been proud of Jesus. Jesus had died for truth. He *was* Truth.

I would have saddened my father because I didn't believe, even after seeing Jesus's miracles and hearing Him speak.

Later, I heard about Christ's resurrection. I fell to my knees, repenting of my disbelief. I had lost time, not knowing Him.

When the disciples met in the upper room after Jesus ascended, I was there. I wouldn't be kept from the truth again. I would wait for it. I would fight for it, just as my Dad had told me. But first, I would know truth.

Time has come and gone. I've come a long way from following the Jewish leaders' traditions. In fact, I proclaimed at the Jerusalem Council that Gentile Christians shouldn't obey Jewish laws.

I had learned my father's lesson, "Know the truth and fight for it. But sometimes fighting means waiting and letting God show them."

Much of my fighting is spent on my knees before God, fighting for my people's hearts, hardened like mine, refusing to believe; fighting for my government, who torture God's people, scattering them to the wind before their persecution; fighting for the truth amidst the added laws of our religious leaders. I fight on my knees to hold onto the God I had for years rejected.

My Brother and my God had lived to show me truth, and had died to give me life. I believe, and I will fight for the truth.

James, brother of Jesus, spent so much time in prayer that it is said "his knees were like those of a camel." The book that bears his name is believed to have been written by him.

Josephus, the Jewish historian, reported that Jewish leaders stoned James to death. Another source said he was thrown from the top of the Temple and beaten to death with a club.

Whichever death he suffered, he died, believing and fighting.

Now he no longer waits to see his God and Savior.

He lives and knows Him.

I am Elizabeth, Wife of Zacharias

MY HUSBAND LOVES me dearly, I know he does. But do you know the heartache of not being able to give him a child? He said I'm enough, but I see the gleam in his eye when he watches the little ones. He loves to bounce his great-nephews and nieces on his knee, or toss them in the air to catch them. He would have made a great dad.

I was never included with the mothers, because I had no child, nor would they listen to my advice. I could only watch them with my wishes unfulfilled and my heart empty.

In a culture where children are your inheritance, and your status is determined by your family size, that put me rather low.

Many times I asked God, "Why?" Or I'd promise Him I would be the best mother ever . . . only to experience being in the womanly way the next month. Did the Lord think I'm unworthy?

Zacharias always comforted me, telling me God had His reasons for my womb being closed.

What important reason could God have had to keep me from having a child? I struggled every month to accept His will. I'd like to say I was godly enough to give it to God once, and then I was fine. But I wasn't.

I'd hold my sisters' and brothers' children in my arms, gaze into their tiny faces, and cry inside.

Everyone assumed, because I had no children, I'd want to do all their extra chores while they were busy with their children. I helped with their little ones. But I longed for my own.

Why did God give that longing, then not give me a child to hold?

Finally all hope was gone, I was past the womanly way. Would we die depending upon Zacharias's nephews to care for us? We would not even die worthy.

Zacharias was loyal and devoted to the Lord, almost to a fault. Always telling me, "God gave us the best." He reminded me the Lord was faithful. I clung to that. Although I had to remind myself every day. You'd think submitting daily to God would get easier. But it didn't.

How could not having a child be the best? But I gave it to God, daily.

Then one day, Zacharias returned from the Temple after performing his priestly duties.

I paused from kneading bread. Why didn't he talk to me? Why was he just motioning with his hands, a strained look on his face? Something was wrong.

He couldn't speak. He told me through signs and writing that God had promised us a son who would foretell of the Coming One.

Redemption for God's people was coming!

I leaned on the bench where I worked. Would we have a son now that my years of childbearing were past? Could I believe God would make my body young again?

I looked at Zacharias for security. How did he feel about it? His eyes danced and sparkled. In fact, he grabbed my flour-covered hands and danced me around the room. I felt in that dance how he, too, had hurt through the years from our lack. Zacharias had mourned my closed womb; now he acted like a boy, excited for feast day.

To think God had opened my womb to give us a child in our old age. We would be blessed like Sarah and Abraham!

In the days that followed, I knew the vision he had seen in the Temple was happening. My body took on a glow that the young mothers had. I could not help but smile when I went to the well to get water and saw young mothers with children. My time had come. The Lord had taken away my disgrace. He had looked with favor upon me.

Yet I could not share my joy. Zacharias's vision at the Temple had been told to everyone. I felt watched by the women. I heard their whispers. They didn't rejoice with me; they felt pity for me. I hid for five months.

I rested much more than I was used to. Many times, I had to stop, even while making a meal. This baby demanded much from my winkled body. My body craved more meats, even fats that I had not wanted for many years. I had to make a longer tunic to reach over my growing middle.

When I was six months along, my niece Mary came to visit. The moment she entered our house, I felt the babe leap in my womb. I heard myself exclaiming, "God has blessed you among women. How has it happened to me, that the mother of my Lord would come to me?"

Mary told of the Child she carried, the Promised One.

The next three months flew as Mary stayed with us. Her family didn't believe her condition was caused by the Lord. But I could look at my growing babe and know the miracles had started. We comforted each other in the midst of the whispers and unbelief of those around us.

When my child came, and it was time to name and circumcise him, I stood by Zacharias, holding our babe. I told the neighbors and relatives, "His name is John."

They ignored me. But at my persistence, they questioned me, "Why wouldn't you name your only child after Zacharias?"

I shook my head.

Finally, they turned to Zacharias asking him, as if to make me see reason.

Zacharias motioned for a tablet to write his wishes.

They all waited, smugly.

Zacharias wrote, "His name is John."

Our family thought we'd lost our senses. "John? Who's named John?"

Once Zacharias had proclaimed his son's name, his tongue was set free. He could speak. He cleared his throat, speaking in a tone no one would question, "His name is John." He made up for the nine months of silence, let me tell you. He praised God. He prophesied of the Coming One.

The people were clearly uneasy. They kept their distance from us, though they spread our news to all the neighbors. Family members in other towns of Judea soon learned about our story. I heard of their whispers, "What will this child be?"

Everyone advised me . . . hold him like this; treat him like that.

I smiled, nodding politely. I had watched many mothers. I knew what to do. Hadn't I promised God in my youth I would be the best mother? But I also knew over the years that I must always rely on God.

The most cherished times were when Zacharias and I would watch him sleep. I'd push back the sweaty lock of dark hair that fell across his face and sing of the Coming One.

John grew. He was different. Not only in how he came to us, but how he grew. He didn't play with other children. He liked being by himself, which was a good thing, because he had no siblings, and we weren't around much of the family.

But I worried about whether he was normal.

Zacharias assured me, "The Lord has His Hand on him. John will shine the light of the Lord into the darkness. He will lead people to know the Coming One."

The neighbors expected something special from him.

I felt pressure to conform to some unwritten standard. How should a child, sent by God, act?

The neighbors accused Zacharias and I of doting on him. "You'll spoil him," they insisted.

I didn't listen. He was my child. We were like grandparents and parents at the same time, giving him all the time and energy we had.

Zacharias bounced John on his knee and threw him in the air.

What if he dropped him? I turned away, unable to watch.

John laughed and begged for more.

When he did fall, I brushed his hair from his forehead and kissed his scrapes away.

Did we dote on him too much? The neighbors thought so.

Zacharias read the Scriptures to John.

And John listened. His heart was tender. He thirsted to know what the Lord had told His people.

John asked questions about the Law and the prophecies of the Coming Messiah.

Zacharias had prophesied that our son would be the man to prepare the way for the Lord.

We were doing all we could to prepare John for that calling. But we also knew God would use him.

As John grew, he didn't make friends. In fact, he confronted his cousin James, the brother of Jesus. He told him, "The Kingdom of God is here in your midst. Repent."

I cautioned him about getting along with people. He didn't want to be disliked by everyone, did he?

Zacharias reminded me, "The Lord made him so." Why did the Lord give me a child who told everyone what they did wrong? He would be disliked. He wouldn't marry. I'd have no grandchildren. Didn't mothers know best? I sighed. I must give him to God. Just like I gave my empty womb to Him.

Zacharias taught him the priestly duties. Wouldn't John take over his role as priest when he was of age? But the more John grew, the more we realized he would not. It disappointed Zacharias. How else could John serve God?

Because we didn't demand he fulfill the priestly duties, we gave the neighbors something more to whisper about us. I tried to ignore their comments, but they hurt.

Zacharias reminded me. "He's the Lord's. Allow God to make John into the man He needs."

Was I holding him too tightly?

When John became a man, he came to me.

I could tell by his expression, he was going to tell me something I wouldn't like. My heart dropped. Tears pooled behind my eyes. I blinked so I could focus on his face.

"Mother, I'm leaving."

It was worse than I thought. "Leaving? Where?"

John shrugged. "To the wilderness."

I scurried to make a lunch for him. As if I could feed him enough for all the days he would stay there.

He laid his hand on my shoulder. "God will provide." He picked up the loaf of bread I had made that morning. "This'll be enough."

I nodded, wiping his hair from his face. I tried to be brave, not to show my tears, but they came unbidden. How could I care for my son in the wilderness?

He turned to Zacharias, who stood at the doorway. Zacharias didn't speak, but hugged him tightly, his face masking the anguish his own heart was feeling.

John hugged him, took one last look around the small house, nodded to us, and turned to leave.

I grabbed his arm. "Take your cloak." I reached up, without thinking, to brush his forehead again. It seemed if I didn't remind him, he would forget to come home. Yet I knew he would not be returning. I choked out, "Shalom."

He smiled, hugged me once more. "Be at peace," he said, and was gone.

How can I "be at peace" when my loved one is not home?

I spent my days listening for news of John.

Whispers had already started that he should have stayed to take care of us in our old age. We were feeling our age. Even making the cooking fire in the morning taxed my hands.

Their accusations were that I hadn't trained him, I should've been stricter. I didn't answer. Why? My heart ached for the son that didn't return. I must give my thoughts to God and allow Him to make things right.

Was his cloak keeping him warm at night? Was he finding shelter from the heat of the day? Was he eating?

Zacharias walked out to the desert himself to see if he could find John. When he returned, one glance at his face told me that he hadn't. He forced a smile. "Be at peace."

Be at peace? When every day I struggle to tell the Lord that John is His! I'd tell Him with my mind and then try to make my heart believe my words. It was hard. How do you give the Lord your son? Every day. Would I call him back from the wilderness and make him a priest? No. Would I want to change him? Sometimes. But he must obey the Lord. My heart wanted to run to the desert and bring him home. My mind reminded me God knew best. I must trust Him. It was a battle every day. I found peace only by giving John back to the One Who gave him to me. Every day.

The days turned to months. I still hoped. I prayed for peace. Could we have heard wrong at his birth?

Then news came from neighbors, returning from selling their sheep. They told of a man preaching by the Jordan River. "He tells anyone who will listen to repent."

I smiled. That sounded like my John. "What else does he say?"

"The Kingdom of God is here." It was John! I knew it was. Only he could survive that wilderness and tell others to repent.

Zacharias and I went to see him. The journey was hard. We had no donkey to carry us. We had to stop many times to rest. Our old bodies weren't what they used to be. I could barely drag my feet along the dirt pathway. Zacharias guided me around ruts in the road. He was as tired as I, but neither one of us would turn back. He asked again if I were able. I nodded, but didn't speak. The effort would required too much energy. We continued, determined to see John.

As we got closer to the Jordan River, we were joined by others, all going to hear this preacher. My steps became lighter. We'd soon see John. We listened to what the people said about him. Were people ready to repent? We joined the people gathered by the river.

A man stood before them, dressed in camel skins, with a leather belt around his waist. This man looked nothing like my John who had left our house. Was it John? I didn't recognize him. He had lost weight. His skin was darkened by the sun. I studied his face under his long beard and hair.

"I am the voice of one crying in the wilderness, make ready the way of the Lord, make His paths straight. Every ravine will be filled, and every mountain will be brought low; the crooked will become straight, and the rough roads smooth and all will see the salvation of God."

I gasped.

Zacharias's hand trembled as he supported my elbow.

His voice was strong, steady . . . and John's! We listened, spellbound, to his words.

A group of men stood at the back, whispering to each other. I recognized them as the scribes and Pharisees from the Temple in Jerusalem. My John had gathered a great following.

John pointed to them. "You brood of vipers. Who warned you to flee from the wrath to come? Bear fruit that shows repentance."

One of them stepped forward in anger. "We have Abraham for our father."

John laughed and shook his head. "God can raise up Abraham's children from these stones."

I trembled and remembered his discussion with James, his cousin. What would these rulers do to John?

Zacharias was squeezing my elbow. He must have forgotten he was holding me.

It hurt. I moved away.

John wasn't finished. "Every tree that doesn't bear good fruit is cut down and thrown into the fire."

One man called, "What should we do?"

John turned his attention to the one who asked. "The man who has two tunics should share with him who has none. He who has food should give to him who has none."

The crowd parted as a tax collector walked up to John. No one wanted even their robes to be touched by such as him. Even as the crowd parted, allowing him to pass, some spat on him, hissing.

He was a Jew, yet he stole from his own people, collecting more taxes than what Rome required. His expensive cloak, tunic, and jewelry spoke of great wealth gained from his greed. He was a traitor to his own people. Bought by Rome.

John saw him.

I held my breath. What would he say to such a man? Especially after condemning the Temple leaders of sin.

The man bowed low before John. He seemed to have forgotten all his wealth, even his position before Rome. "Teacher, I want to be baptized."

The crowd gasped.

John didn't hesitate. He reached for his hand and led him into that fast-flowing, dirty river and submerged him.

When they reached the shore again, the man embraced John, kissing him on both cheeks. They both dripped with water. "Teacher, what shall I do?"

John smiled. "Collect no more than what you are told."

The man nodded. He turned to the group of tax collectors who had come with him. "Let's do the things he has said."

Only the Spirit of the Most High could change the hardened heart of a tax collector and make him give up his money. Truly deliverance of men's hearts had come!

John feared no man. He spoke God's truth. Because of John's words, this man had repented and was changed.

I remembered all the neighbors' whisperings at how wrong Zacharias and I had been in our training. My heart filled with joy. We had followed the Lord. We had trained John right. And now John was pointing people to the Most High.

The tax collector's repentance stirred a group of soldiers. One yelled, "What about us, what should we do?"

Were they hecklers, testing John's words? I could feel the blood drain from my face.

But John didn't hesitate. "Don't take money from anyone by force, or accuse anyone falsely. Be content with your wages." Soldiers were known to accuse Jews falsely. Their wages were close to poverty level, but they often supplemented them by taking from the Jews.

The soldier didn't scoff at John's words, but considered them.

Zacharias whispered in my ear, "Truly the Spirit of the Lord is in our midst."

We listened, spellbound, not only because it was our son who shared the Words of the Lord, but because his words changed lives.

The crowd watched, expecting something. Whispers passed among them. "Is this the Christ?"

As if he heard them, John spoke, "I am not the Christ."

One Pharisee shouted, "Who are you then? Elijah?"

"I'm not."

"A prophet?"

"No."

"Who then? So we can answer those who sent us."

John raised his arm to heaven. "I'm the voice of one crying in the wilderness, 'Make the Lord's way straight.'"

The Pharisee confronted him, "Why do you baptize, if you're not a prophet?"

John answered, "I baptize with water, but One is coming who is mightier than I. I'm not fit to remove His sandals. He will baptize with the Holy Spirit and fire. He will gather His own, but burn those who are not His."

My heart wasn't big enough for my joy. The Desired One was coming! And we had been privileged to help prepare John for the Lord's work.

The people were hungry to hear the Lord's Words.

Even though the words were the Lord's, my mother's heart wanted to tell him, "Soften your words. Don't stir up anger." But I knew that was my way, not the Lord's. I asked God to give me peace, especially when I thought of what could happen to John when he angered certain men. I glanced back at the religious rulers.

They would report to those in Jerusalem. It wouldn't go well for John if he ever stepped inside the Temple.

I almost laughed out loud.

John wouldn't enter the Temple . . . he looked like a mad man. He wouldn't be allowed even on the stairs of the holy Temple.

What did that say of the Temple, when the man God sent couldn't enter the place where God was to be worshipped?

I thought about the many times Zacharias and I had tried to make John a priest. That was not God's Way. John was proclaiming the words of the Lord. The Lord's ways weren't my ways.

As we listened and watched, one man stepped forward. He looked familiar. Was that Mary's Son?

John hesitated. Had he lost confidence?

I strained to hear him.

John seemed confused. "You're mightier than I. I'm not fit to untie your sandals. I need to be baptized by You, and yet You come to me?"

Jesus bowed. "This fulfills all righteousness."

John turned to the crowd. "Behold, the Lamb of God Who takes away the sin of the world! He is higher in rank than I, for He existed before me. I testify that this is the Son of God."

I watched my son baptize the Son of God. God knew how to make a mom's heart complete. I glanced at Zacharias. His shoulders were back as straight as a soldier's. The Lord had chosen to use us to bring his forerunner into the world and train him to be His spokesman.

As we watched, a dove flew from a nearby tree to land on Jesus as he came out of the water.

The crowd gasped.

Before we had time to wonder at what it might mean, thunder sounded. There wasn't a cloud in the sky, but the sky rumbled like thunder, only it was a voice, God's voice. I looked at the sky and could see only the sun shining directly on Jesus. Words came out of the thunder; saying, "You are My beloved Son. In You I am well-pleased."

I fell to my knees on the sand before this voice and worshipped. Our Deliver had come.

Around me others also fell. Zacharias with me. I knew we would both struggle to rise from our knees, but I knew our worship had just begun.

Others from the crowd helped us stand to our feet. When I stood, I happened to glance to the back where the rulers had stood.

They remained on their feet, their faces reflecting the darkness in their hearts. I shivered, in spite of the warmth of the day, and wondered what they could say to such miracles and truth. I didn't have long to wait.

At the end of the day, we followed John to a little cove away from the crowds. We met his disciples and ate with them. While he taught them, Jesus walked by. John pointed again and said, "Behold, the Lamb of God." Two of his disciples left John and followed Jesus.

I felt hurt, "Why didn't they stay with you?"

John corrected me. "Mom, they follow the Christ!"

I nodded, quick to acknowledge my hasty mouth. It was my mother's heart talking and not my mind. We traveled home. Satisfied. Glad for the trip, but weary.

It was hard to be content with the day's routine after seeing John and Jesus. I listened for news.

When the Jordan River was low, we heard of John spending time in Aenon near Salim, where there was enough water. John seemed to be losing popularity. I asked Zacharias about it.

"Elizabeth, he's not the Christ. He is sent ahead of Him. I spoke with him before we left. He understood his role. He told me Jesus must increase and he must decrease. Our son has done his job. He doesn't seek followers. He points them to the Desired One."

I nodded. That was true. It was a mother's heart again, hurting for her son.

I worried over John's outspokenness. Who would he anger who would cause him harm? I didn't have long to wonder.

I was at the town well, filling my vessel. I had paused, gathering strength to lift the water to my shoulder. Sometimes I wished Zacharias could get the water, my bones did ache so.

The neighbor woman came hurrying to the well. "Elizabeth, have you heard?"

Of course, I hadn't heard, and I probably didn't want to hear, but I couldn't lift the water.

"John has finally said too much. You should have trained him not to speak so boldly."

Now, I didn't want to move. "My John? What have you heard?"

"He spoke against King Herod, accusing him of his sins."

I dropped the vessel. The water poured down my leg. "What has happened?"

"Herod has John in prison."

I sat there unable to move. John had spoken only truth. All the Jews knew of Herod's evil. He had recently taken his brother's wife as his own. And now, he had my John.

The woman looked at me. "Elizabeth, you really must go home! You're all wet. Look at your tunic!"

I looked down, but didn't see. All I could see was my son in prison.

I don't know how I managed to go home that day. I don't even remember if I brought my water vessel.

Zacharias listened with quiet acceptance when I told him the news. Almost as if he had expected it.

I clung to him, hoping after I cried I'd find out it was just a bad dream. It was not.

We listened for news, hoping John's life would be spared.

He would never change his words. He spoke the truth with boldness.

Herod questioned him. He listened to him preach. Would Herod grant his freedom?

News gave me little hope. It seemed only a matter of time.

We prayed.

I avoided the well when others were there, yet I wanted to hear any news. I was torn to know, yet I didn't want to know.

Before the news reached us, I knew in my heart. I felt it.

The neighbor brought news, confirming what I already felt, "Herod gave a party. He promised to grant his wife's daughter any wish. She asked for John's head."

John's head. I thought of those curls I had brushed from his infant face while he slept. Of that stubborn lock of hair that fell over his eyes whenever he bent over his reading. Of his long hair from living in the wilderness. I would touch it now, if only I could.

The news jarred Zacharias. He never rose from the bench, where he received the news. He slumped forward onto the table.

After the sun had set and the room had grown quite dark, I spoke to him. When he didn't answer, I lit a candle and touched him. Zacharias was gone.

How is a mother to live longer than her son? How would I continue without my husband? Although old, we weren't supposed to die of a broken heart. We were to die with satisfaction and in peace. . . . Hadn't the Lord promised John would be the forerunner of deliverance? I sat beside Zacharias, as if he could still bring me security and comfort. I held his hand, even though there was no warmth in it.

I understood the coming of the Desired One better. He would make restoration complete. He would give us new life. I would again see Zacharias and my John one day. We would be together, and at peace. But first, the Coming One must do His work.

As I bowed my head in submission to the will of the Lord, I was grateful to have a mother's part in bringing the news to a waiting world. But a mother's heart is not without pain. I linger, when those I love have gone on. But I look to the Coming One, Who will give, even this old mom, peace. He will bring redemption and make all things right.

I am Judas Iscariot

—— ⚜ ——

MANY WOULD SAY that Iscariot stands for Sicarii, an extremist group of Jewish Zealots who undermine the Roman occupation of Judea. I won't tell you whether or not I hold a dagger in my cloak to kill a passerby without warning.

But I will tell you a story that changed my life.

News reached me of a man preaching throughout Galilee about the coming Kingdom. He could expel the Romans from our country. He was gaining a following, under the deception of peace and healing.

I went to hear him. When I saw the Man could heal all diseases, I thought my father would be pleased with me for bringing him the news. "I saw a Man who can heal you."

He spat at me. "A leper is cursed for life."

But he came.

As we followed the crowds, I remembered my father as a Pharisee of high standing.

My father held up the Law as a standard I could never meet. The Law he disciplined by didn't make me clean. It showed me the depths of my depravity. I could never be acceptable. I felt his disappointment in his beatings; I saw the regret in his eyes. I was his only son, yet I failed him.

Now, by the Law's standard, he had been removed from the Temple and from his house, because of his leprosy. Now he was receiving from the Law what he had always meted out to me.

That was years ago, and by now the leprosy had changed his body, but it hadn't changed how he controlled people with the Law.

My thoughts were interrupted as we neared the Healer.

The Man didn't ask questions; He just reached out and healed my father and told him to go to the priest to be declared "clean."

How ironic that my father had once declared men clean or unclean when he had ruled in the Temple. Now he must go to the Temple and be declared clean by another.

I walked beside my father as he returned to the Temple. I waited for him to thank me for taking him to the Healer.

He did not.

I continued to follow the Man. It was said He would remove the yoke of Roman bonds from our shoulders. But this man didn't prepare armies, nor stir up the people with hate. He talked of giving to the poor and loving your enemies.

I listened, waiting for His actions to be inconsistent with His words.

They weren't.

I wanted to condemn Him, to prove that nobody's perfect. So I kept on following Him wherever He went, watching.

He chose his disciples, mostly those who lived near Galilee, where He was from. They were a rowdy bunch; fishermen who lived a rough lives.

But Jesus also chose *me*. I had never been chosen for anything. My father refused to make me a priest, so I had been joined the Zealots. But they didn't really want me either, unless I could prove my alligiance by killing. Jesus invited me personally into His inner circle.

None of the other disciples knew me. I was from Kerioth, a city of Judah. I kept quiet and listened. I was educated. I knew the Law. They respected me . . . accepted me. I belonged somewhere for the first time in my life.

People gave Jesus money, a token for His words, appreciation for his healing. He received a lot. My father should take lessons from Jesus on how to get the people's money. He didn't beg or demand. People gave out of . . . was it love?

My hand brushed against my purse, tied to my cloak's belt. It rattled.

The disciples had made me their treasurer. (If my father could see me now!) They misread my quietness for integrity, my education for wisdom. I spoke of giving to the poor. Who wouldn't want to help the poor? But who is poor? Wasn't I? I found the extra money helpful.

Being treasurer gave me freedom that the other disciples didn't have. I went as I pleased. They assumed I was getting food or giving to the poor. I laughed. They were easily deceived.

Jesus treated me like the others. He accepted me for who I was. He made me feel I had worth.

It gave me hope that I might even gain acceptance from my own father. I approached him with what he valued: the Law. I told him that Jesus's disciples didn't wash their hands before eating. I laughed when I saw him listening to Jesus soon afterward.

He confronted Jesus, "Your disciples eat with unwashed hands."

Instead of correcting His disciples, Jesus defended them. "It is not what enters into the mouth that defiles the man, but what proceeds out of the mouth is what defiles the man." Jesus then confronted my father, You demand money for the Temple, instead of allowing the people to honor and take care of their parents."

I glanced at my father. He was livid!

"You hypocrite! You elevate your traditions and money over the Law."

Maybe Jesus didn't know who he was talking to. I nudged Him. "You've offended the Pharisees."

Jesus brushed me aside and stared at my father. "He is blind, leading the blind. Both will fall into a pit."

I shrugged. I had warned Him. He would experience the anger of my father. I waited for my father to explode.

His neck veins bulged. He glanced at the crowd. What could he say to what he knew was the truth? And yet, he must maintain his authority. I could only smile at what he would do when he reached home and took it out on the servants. At least I hadn't caused it this time.

Jesus's words matched His life. He didn't expect to be treated special because of His position as our leader; in fact, He served us.

I waited for Him to fail. He did not.

Initially, I thought I had deceived Jesus. I thought He was too naïve to distrust me. I stole and laughed at His simplicity. When I found out He knew and hadn't said anything or tried to punish me, I found He was weak and didn't dare to confront me. In time, I realized He really believed in the peace He spoke about. I knew then He would never cause an uprising against Rome.

When I stopped at my father's house on one of our travels, my father asked me. "Why do you stay with Him? He won't overthrow Rome. He's not the Man we seek."

My father couldn't control Him. Jesus didn't cower before him. That made my father hate Him. But why did I stay with Him?

Maybe because He seemed real. He cared for me. I shrugged. "What will the elders do with Him?"

"Remove Him."

As if Jesus was some fly to be removed! I recognized the look on my faither's face. He would stop at nothing until Jesus was destroyed.

Another time when I stopped at the house, I told my father, "Jesus knows your plans. . . to deliver Him to the Roman courts."

"How could He, unless you told him?"

I shook my head. I hadn't. I wouldn't take the blame either. Jesus had pronounced woes on all the Temple's leaders. I stood up to my father, recounting them. "He said you were clean on the outside, like a cup, but full of robbery and self-indulgence on the inside. He called you whitewashed tombs . . . beautiful on the outside, but full of dead men's bones and uncleanness." I tried not to smile. Jesus had described my father well. I was beginning to see the same thing.

I should have been ready when my father slapped me. I responded, not by cowering like I would have done as a boy, but by confronting him. "I find His words true."

The truth of this Man infuriated my father. I didn't have to lie. I could fight with truth and win.

My father calmed himself. He needed me to inform him of Jesus's whereabouts. He depended upon my inside information. After slapping me, he calmed down. "Tell me what He does."

I shrugged. "Invite Him to dinner. You could question Jesus personally. Perhaps even take Him, then."

My father smiled. He liked my plan.

When I returned to Jesus, I felt the weight of my deception. The disciples didn't even glance up as I settled among them. They took my absence as giving to the poor. They thought I was someone I wasn't.

But Jesus looked at me. He waited until I looked Him in the eye.

I cringed. How could He make me feel unclean, when all I had done was argue with my father? Or was that another lie? Did I lie so much I didn't even know the truth? Being around Jesus made me test my words against His truth. I came up lacking. I looked down from His gaze. Why did I care what Jesus thought of me?

Later when we were walking to another city, I walked beside Jesus. "About the other night, when I was gone . . ." Why did I feel I must explain to Him what I did? He held no power over me. "Why do You think You'll be killed?"

Jesus shook his head. "Judas, why couldn't you cure the boy who was controlled by demons?"

At first, I thought he was talking about my boyhood—the demons that followed me from my father. But then I shivered, remembering that afternoon a couple weeks back. A father had brought his son to Andrew, Peter, and I. He begged us to heal him. The boy threw himself into our cook fire. It took all of us to pull him from the flames. Even then, the boy beat us. I shook my head. "Where did he get his power to throw off four grown men?"

Jesus persisted. "By what power did I cure him?"

"If you have power to control demons, then how could men kill you?"

The only time I remember being touched by my father was when he beat me. Jesus usually didn't touch me. I kept myself aloof. But Jesus touched me now. "Because I allow them to."

I didn't cringe from His touch, which surprised me. His touch showed me the answer better than any words He could have spoken. Why would His love allow man to kill him? What purpose would it serve? I didn't understand.

When we came into Capernaum, Peter was accosted by the tax-collectors, asking for the two-drachma tax. Peter responded like he always did, without thinking, "We already paid it."

Before I could tell him we hadn't paid it, Jesus asked, "Who do kings collect taxes from, their sons or strangers?"

Peter answered, "From strangers."

Jesus nodded. "Even so, we won't offend them. Throw in a fishing line and take the first fish you catch. Look in its mouth. You'll find a shekel. Give it to the tax collector for you and me."

I laughed. Would Peter actually believe His story? I knew enough about telling lies to know this was a big one. One worthy of a good laugh. I followed Peter. When he brought the first fish in, he pulled out a shekel from the fish's mouth. I asked to see the money. Now that was another way my father could make more money!

It left me disappointed. Did Jesus speak only the truth? How did He know the truth?

I didn't believe my father would have us for dinner, so when he invited us, I was surprised.

Jesus had told us He would be crucified. That had to be a Roman execution. What accusation did my father have that would warrant a Roman trial? I took my father into another room. "What plans do you have?"

He shook his head. "Not here."

I watched my father's expression. "He said He'd be crucified."

When my father gasped, I knew it was true. "How does He know?"

I watched the table where Jesus lay.

My father grabbed my arm. "You are still with us. Aren't you?"

I turned back to stare at him. "Crucify him? Father! Is that how you get rid of someone you can't answer? His truth makes me wonder about all you taught me."

My father swallowed. "You question me?"

I laughed at his inconsistency. "Isn't that what you taught? That we shouldn't honor our fathers, but give to the Temple. Now I don't honor you, nor give to the Temple. Your traditions are burdensome. They bind people under your control."

My father looked into the room with his guests and gasped.

I followed his look. Was that the woman from down the street? The one that used to come to my father's chamber? "Seems like Jesus is not only disrobing you of your priestly authority, but also taking your entertainment from your chamber."

My father smacked me. He glanced into the room to see if others had heard. "We will speak later."

I refused to rub my face. "I look forward to it."

I led the way back into the room with Jesus and the disciples. The cushions on the floor allowed the circle to widen. I squeezed in beside Jesus. This dinner would be interesting.

The woman sat at Jesus's feet, weeping and wiping his feet with her unbound hair.

My father slid in beside Jesus on His other side. He lowered his voice. "If you knew what kind of woman you allowed to kiss your feet, you wouldn't allow her to touch you."

I almost grunted out loud. The Pharisees had caught a woman in adultery. They had thrown her at Jesus's feet and asked if she should be stoned. Surely they knew there had to be two guilty parties! But now my father, in trying so hard to trap Jesus, was as good as admitting to sinning with this woman.

Jesus didn't even address her sin. "Simon. You invited me to your house but didn't greet me with a kiss, yet she has not stopped kissing my feet. You didn't wash my feet when I entered your house, yet she hasn't stopped washing my feet with her hair. You offered me a token of hospitality, yet she has given me her heart."

While Jesus spoke, she took from her tunic's pocket a vial of perfume. She poured it on Jesus's head.

I leaned toward Jesus. "Why did she waste this perfume? She could have sold it for three hundred denarii and given the money to the poor."

Jesus didn't speak only to me, He raised His voice so all could hear. "Leave her be. She's done a good deed. You'll always have the poor with you; but you won't always have Me. She prepares Me for burial. Wherever the gospel is preached, this deed will be spoken of in memory of her."

I finished the dinner in silence. What had I done worthy of remembering?

The following day, I met with the rulers and chief priests at the Temple. When I entered the room, they stopped talking. I approached the chief priest. Should I have come? I saw my father sitting behind the chief priest. He glowed with pride. I'd never seen him look at me before like that. He even smiled at me. I stood taller and faced the chief priest. "I will turn Him over to you. What will you give me?"

The council agreed. "Thirty pieces of silver."

I nodded and left. I thought if I pleased my father, I would finally feel worthy, accepted, loved. My decision to turn Jesus over to them would fulfill what Jesus already knew would happen.

How would Jesus escape? I had seen Him disappear before when they would have cast him over a cliff. This would be a miracle worth watching.

I would use the money to help Him escape the Romans' power. Even as I planned, my insides churned. I couldn't eat. Was this right? But even Jesus said it would happen.

I ignored my doubts and looked for an opportunity to turn Jesus over to the rulers.

It was Passover. That would be a perfect time for the rulers to take Him. There would be no crowds.

But Jesus wouldn't tell me where we were having the meal, even though I asked Him several times. I asked the other disciples. No one knew. He didn't tell anyone. He sent two disciples ahead of us to prepare the meal.

When we arrived, there were no servants at the door to wash our feet. There was no one I could send with a message to my father.

No crowds knew where we were. This would be ideal. I tried to leave to tell the rulers.

As I considered, Jesus began washing my feet.

I felt uncomfortable. "Teacher, You wash my feet?"

How could I turn him over to the rulers, after He served me like this?

Jesus just nodded. He wouldn't look at my face but went around the circle to all of us. When He came to Peter, Peter wouldn't allow Him to touch his feet.

I shook my head. Peter would never be a ruler. He must learn how to be served.

Then Jesus told us about serving.

He wouldn't free us from Roman rule. Romans didn't understand serving, nor did my father. Neither did I. Why did I continue to follow Jesus? He had a way of drawing me. He seemed to know my thoughts.

I shivered, determining to do what I had promised.

When He finished washing our feet, Jesus settled on the cushions for the meal. He seemed subdued, withdrawn. He spoke softly, "One of you will betray Me."

All of us looked around the circle. "Is it I?"

I had not considered what I was doing as betraying Him. I was only facilitating what He said would happen. His power would prove greater than my father's. His power would save Him. I asked with the others, "Surely, it's not I, Teacher?"

Jesus nodded. No one else heard when he answered, "You've said it yourself."

How did He know? I had been careful.

Peter gestured to John, who leaned on Jesus's bosom, "Tell us who it is."

Jesus answered, "I'll give the bread to him. The Son of Man is to go, just as the Law says, but woe to that man who betrays the Son of Man! It would've been better for that man, if he hadn't been born."

Jesus handed the piece of bread to me. I took it, but could not eat. How dare He curse me! How did He know it was me? What had I done for Him to know? I went over my actions. Nothing could have given me away.

I couldn't please my father and please Jesus at the same time. Shouldn't I honor my father? Isn't that what Jesus even said? My lies took over.

A dispute broke out among the disciples about who would be greatest in Jesus's kingdom. I sighed. These ignorant fishermen expected to rule? I had more inborn authority than any of them.

Jesus silenced them. "The one who is the greatest must become like a servant. Just as My Father gave Me the Kingdom, I grant you food and drink at My table in My Kingdom."

I sighed. No ruler served. How could He rise against Rome with this plan?

Jesus told me in a tone of resignation, "What you do, do quickly."

I glanced around. No one else knew why He told me that. I frequently left to take care of their food and shelter. They would assum I was leaving for those reasons now.

Jesus knew otherwise.

I felt guilty as I stood to leave. I wondered if I had ever truly deceived Him. Had He seen through all those times when the money was short? He hadn't confronted me even when we'd had to eat from a stranger's wheat on the Sabbath. I felt the blood leave my face, realizing He knew even the thoughts of my heart. I laid down the bread He'd given me, uneaten, and left.

When I stepped outside, I wrapped my cloak more tightly around me against the coolness of the evening. Would I find the rulers before Jesus left here? I ran through the streets, hurrying to get this done before my mind convinced me not to finish the job. My father's words raced through my mind, "You're worthless, never able to finish a job." I would complete this job. I would please my father. And Jesus would work one of His miracles and escape the hands of the Romans. His Kingdom would come.

I reached my father's house.

He was annoyed with my interruption of his feast.

"I've come to tell you where Jesus is."

His entire demeanor changed. He was willing to delay celebrating Passover for this. He sent servants to tell the other rulers and requested officers and a Roman cohort of six-hundred men.

I gulped. Jesus's miracle would have to be great. When we arrived at the house where we had eaten the meal, Jesus and the disciples weren't there.

Though I hadn't eaten, my gut churned. I must find Jesus tonight. "He often took us over the ravine of the Kidron where there's a garden." I led the way. They carried lanterns and torches. I glanced at the Roman leader at my side. Weren't we trying to overthrow the Romans? Why would we use them for our purposes? They followed me, their lights showing the path in the moonless night.

I saw Jesus from a distance, His little group of disciples hovering around Him as we came close.

I lagged behind the officers as we approached. They all held clubs and swords. Would they act like a mob?

Jesus stepped into the circle of light from our torches. "Whom do you seek?"

The commander spoke, "Jesus, the Nazarene."

"I am He."

The Romans soldiers fell back.

Jesus saw me, as I hid amongst the soldiers. "Friend, do what you have come for."

Jesus still called me friend. I tripped as I stepped forward and kissed Him on the cheek.

The soldiers surrounded him.

They treated Him like a criminal. This was not what I thought they would do. Why didn't Jesus do something?

The soldiers stood, waiting for a command.

Peter drew his sword and struck at a servant who stood beside me.

The soldiers grabbed Peter, bringing him forward to be taken as well.

Jesus spoke to Peter, "Put away your sword. Shouldn't I drink of the cup the Father gives?" He bent in the dirt, and retrieved the man's ear. He held it to the man's head. The ear was restored.

He commanded, "You only want Me. Let these others go."

The commander nodded to his men, and they released Peter. But they bound Jesus's hands and took Him away.

Wouldn't He show His power and prevent the soldiers from taking Him? Had He lost His power? Why didn't He fight? I didn't understand. He had the power to overthrow these men. Why didn't He use it?

Before I was out of the circle of light, He turned one last time and looked at me.

His look told me; He accepted my betrayal. He accepted even death.

I didn't understand. Show Your power! My mind screamed, but no words came out. When I couldn't see the lights from their torches, I ran to the Temple where the elders would meet me. My heart raced as the image of Jesus's hands bound behind Him lingered in my mind.

The passageway of the Temple was dark, lit only by the scones on the walls. I wished to be done with this whole thing. I stumbled into the room, pausing at the doorway. They all sat waiting. One was lighting a candle on a table in the middle of the assembly. Had they been sitting in the dark? I looked around the circle of leaders, the flickering light from the candle casting eerie reflections on each face. "Where's the silver?"

The leader took his time opening the chest containing the people's tithes and offerings. He counted out the silver.

Hurry up! My thoughts screamed. I shifted from foot to foot. The sooner I left this room, the better I'd feel. I licked my lips, conscious of the silver accumulating in front of him. When thirty pieces of silver had been counted out on the table. I grabbed them, dumping them into my purse, and pulling the drawstring closed. I secured it in the folds of my cloak. It was heavy. Keeping my hand on the bottom of my purse, I held its contents. It could tear my pocket, or be visible to a thief.

I walked to the doorway and looked back at my father. I nodded, then left. I could not run now, because the coins clanged too noisily. But I hurried to my father's house. I went to my chamber, still available even though I had been gone many years. I removed a tile from the floor; then stuffed the entire purse into the hole and replaced the loose tile. I breathed heavily as I considered.

Where should I go? Where would the disciples go? I had spent the last three years following Jesus. Now I felt like a lost son, unable to go home. I laughed, but it sounded hollow even in my chamber. I was home, but felt abandoned.

Why hadn't Jesus shown His power and usurped the Roman soldiers before they took him? Did He really mean to die?

The thought caught me by surprise.

What had I done?

I paced, stepping on the tile that hid the blood-money. I had given the only man who had ever loved me to the power of the hated Romans. I was worse than a tax-collector.

I had stabbed people to stir up hate against the Romans. I had followed Jesus because He told of a new Kingdom. Jesus talked about freedom, peace, life. Isn't that what He promised? Isn't that what I fought for? Why didn't He make it happen? When He spoke, even demons listened. Surely the Romans weren't stronger than a demons!

I couldn't shake the image of Jesus with his hands tied behind his back.

My pacing took on a frantic speed, as if I could outrun my thoughts.

I thought about all the times Jesus had made me feel worthy. Loved. His words that one would betray Him echoed in my mind. Those were strong words. I didn't betray Him.

"What you do, do quickly. Quickly. Quickly . . . ." I pulled my hair and tore my tunic.

What had I done?

I knew what the Romans would do to a man.

Had I handed Jesus to them for that?

It was early morning when I finally decided what I should do. I retrieved my purse from its hiding place and returned to the council. They were still meeting. I was relieved, but I was too preoccupied to wonder why. They didn't hold trial before morning sacrifices, nor would they execute a man before the Passover.

When I stepped into the room, the chief priest demanded, "What do you want?"

I tried to speak, but couldn't. I coughed, clearing my throat. "I've sinned by betraying innocent blood." I couldn't look at my father. I didn't want to see his rejection and disappointment in me, again. All I could still see was Jesus's final look at me.

The chief priest shrugged, not even considering my words. "What is that to us?"

I looked around the circle of men. Not one of them really listened to me. I couldn't undo my deed. I saw it in their faces. In frantic desperation, I opened my purse and dumped the coins on the floor. The money that once gave me the feeling of control and power, now felt hot and unclean. Money couldn't buy peace. Money couldn't bring back one Man's innocent life. The coins rolled across the floor. Before they stopped rolling, I left.

I had sinned. I couldn't rationalize my lies nor undo them. I couldn't deceive my father. I hadn't deceived Jesus. And I could no longer deceive myself. I was undone, with no hope.

I don't remember walking to the garden where Jesus spent time with us. It was there He had told us of His Kingdom, of a place He was preparing for His own. He warned of false teachers, telling lies that didn't match with what He said, using the Law and adding to it. I could see the disciples sitting around Him, asking questions. His answers gave peace.

Where was the peace now? What had I done to the Teacher?

The image of His bound hands pounded in my mind. "What you do, do quickly . . . ." A donkey stood tied to a tree nearby. Was it the donkey that had brought Jesus into the city a week ago? All I could see was Jesus bound, turned over to the Romans. He was innocent. He would die. It was my fault.

I grabbed the rope off the donkey. I found the nearest tree that overhung the ravine. I climbed a branch and tied the end to it. I would end my life, rather than see what my actions had brought.

I could not please my father, but neither had I pleased Jesus. My life was cursed. I would no longer see the disappointment in the eyes of Jesus. I had tried to outlive my father's disappointment. But it clung to me. Always reaching for approval, I had never attained it. I was fulfilling my father's statement. I was good for nothing, never finishing a task.

Could I have found that acceptance in Jesus? He had given me worth. But I had chosen to betray Him. I was cursed, even in His sight. What hope did I have of finding acceptance? Jesus couldn't save people from the bondage of their own lies and deceit, could He? Or was that another lie? Would Jesus offer forgiveness to me? No. I shook my head. He had cursed me.

I looped the other end of the rope around my neck and jumped.

I am Simon, the Leper

———— ✦ ————

IWAS A PHARISEE of high standing, well-respected, serving in the Temple.

Watching the people give their gifts and sacrifices at the Temple, I instructed one hesitant giver to give more. He excused his meager offering by saying he must care for his ailing father. I rebuked him. His offering to God must take priority over his parents. The man seemed torn between obeying my words and the need to honor his parents.

A disturbance at the entrance of the Temple caught my attention. The crowd parted, like the waves of the Jordan when we entered our Promised Land. A leper had entered, against all rules and policy. He was unclean.

I must rid the Temple of this man. I called the Roman guards, standing outside the Temple.

They entered boldly, but wouldn't touch him.

The leper begged to be allowed a sacrifice for his sin. He wanted to be cleansed.

No sacrifice could cover the sin of defiling the Temple!

Finally, in my anger, seeing no one obeyed me, I threw him out of the Temple myself.

The man rolled down the Temple stairs and lay still at the bottom, his legs bent awkwardly underneath him.

No one stepped forward to help him. Time seemed suspended, until I shook myself and demanded a peasant remove him.

He stooped unwillingly to lift the him, but jerked backwards. He looked at me with anger, accusing me with his look. "He is dead."

The shock of the news left my mouth dry. He wasn't *that* frail. Hadn't he withstood the soldiers and all the people when he had entered the Temple?

After the initial shock passed, anger took over. How could a man, so unclean, dare enter God's house! This was God's judgment on him for bringing uncleanness into the Temple. He deserved to die. God had cleansed His Temple.

I looked around. What would the other leaders think of my actions?

They had already turned back to their duties.

I breathed a sigh of relief. I wouldn't be held accountable for this man's blood.

He had brought it on his own back by entering the Temple unclean.

I directed the same peasant to remove him from the city. He didn't dare refuse. If he didn't obey, he would be excommunicated from the Temple.

I fingered a widow's mite, worth only a fraction of a copper coin, in my tunic pocket. "Here." I said, as I tossed the coin to him.

He caught it, studied it a moment, and frowned. Then, glancing once more at the body, he dragged the man toward the gate of the city.

As soon as he was out of sight, I excused my departure and ran home.

I ordered servants, "Bring water to my chamber." I bathed seven times, ordering the water hotter each time and using oils to ensure I would be clean.

As I waited to be done with the purification period required by the Law, I could not sleep. Each morning, I examined every inch of skin to see if any had changed.

One week went by. This day I could declare I was clean, according to the Law. I examined my skin, more as a duty, than as the frantic searching I had done on those first days of waiting. When I saw my white finger, I screamed. I scrubbed again, but I couldn't remove the whiteness.

I was unclean. I could do nothing. How could I be a leper? I was a Pharisee, clean, and in God's service. What would I do?

The sun rose overhead. I saw through my window the Temple where I had served since my youth as a respected man of the Most High God. How could someone so clean, now be declared unclean?

I sat all day, denying my condition.

My son entered my chamber. I ordered him to leave, but not before I saw his eyes widen as he stared at my whitened finger.

I hid it in the folds of my robe, too late.

The sun was setting.

I heard a commotion in the hallway.

Armed soldiers barged into my room.

I stood against them. "What's the meaning of this?"

They grabbed me by the arms, dragging me from my house.

I turned back to glimpse my son standing behind them, watching. I spat at him. "You're no son of mine. I am *clean*."

He watched those soldiers take me away from my own house.

I yelled, "You'll be sorry when God judges you. I'm clean. Do you hear me? I am clean!"

They dragged me through the streets of the city in shame, as if I was a common criminal, worthy of disgrace.

I bowed my head, hoping no one would recognize me.

The city gates were closing when we reached them. "Wait!" One of the soldiers called, "We have one that must be removed."

The gate keeper opened the gate wide for us.

They threw me to the ground by the side of the road outside the city. They wiped their hands on their tunics and hurried through the gate before it closed.

I watched in the light of the setting sun, as the doors swung shut, clanging loudly. I heard the bar drop in place across the gate.

I would hear that noise every night for years afterward. The gate that kept me out of my own city.

I was a leper. I was alone. I was unclean.

The disgrace of my condition didn't fully settle over me until morning. The gates opened as the sun rose.

A servant from my house brought me a basket of bread and drink. She dropped the basket, bowed quickly, and left, not even glancing back.

I wrapped my robe around my body and hid my fingers in its sleeve. Was this what it was like to be unclean? To be unacceptable in everyone's eyes? To be stared at like a freak and a misfit? Or ignored like I didn't exist?

I grabbed the basket and lifted the linen napkin. I brought the wineskin to my lips. I hadn't realized how thirsty I was. I hadn't eaten nor drunk anything the day before. I choked as I tasted the liquid. Spitting it out and throwing the wineskin to the ground, I watched the contents pour out on the dirt. They give me water! I am a Pharisee of the highest order. I deserve the best of wines with my meals. I licked my lips and grabbed for the wineskin, almost empty. Water was better than nothing.

The sun grew hot. I stayed under a group of trees outside the gate. I wouldn't beg in the streets to be cast out in public disgrace. Nor would I live with the other lepers hiding in caves.

My son, Judas, came. He seemed apologetic, hesitant to speak.

I cursed him for calling the Roman soldiers. I cursed him for all his faults.

His look of concern turned to hardness as I spoke, as if he didn't care about his sins. He shrugged. "Father, it's the Law." He backed away, finally walking back into the city. He had thrown his own father out of his house!

Days melted into years. My fingers were not the only thing that turned white. Whiteness crept up my arms, covering my toes, feet, and legs. I could feel holes in my face. Just as the disease crept through my skin, anger seeped into my heart. My anger spilled over onto anyone who came close.

The servants still brought my daily portion of bread and water. Never did they bring wine.

One day, I sat against a tree as my son approached. I had already received my daily food. Why had he come? I watched his approach through semi-closed eyes.

He bowed before me.

"What do you want?" I growled, angry at his beggardly posture. Couldn't he at least stand tall like the son of a man of power?

He licked his lips and looked at the ground in front of me. "A Man from Galilee has been teaching in the synagogues and proclaiming the gospel of the Kingdom."

"Why do the Pharisees allow him in the synagogues?"

Judas fidgeted. "He speaks with authority." He gathered his cloak more tightly around him, as if to give him confidence. "He heals."

I spat at his feet. "A leper is cursed for life."

He continued as if he hadn't heard. "He heals all kinds of sickness. I went to see Him. He can heal you, Father."

I listened, but didn't believe. I had watched the whiteness take over my body. I was disfigured. Did I dare hope?

He squatted down and looked me in the eyes. "Come, see, Father."

We went to find this Man Who could work miracles. Would this Man touch a leper and heal him?

We met Him as He came down from a mountain outside the city.

The crowds parted, allowing me to walk right up to him. They moved aside out of fear of the dreaded disease.

I bowed before Him. "Lord, if You're willing, You can make me clean."

He didn't hesitate. He stretched out His hand and touched me. "I'm willing; be clean."

I hadn't been touched in years! His touch cleaned the inside of me and left me whole outside. I looked at my hands, my feet . . . the whiteness was gone! I touched my face. The holes had closed.

He still held my shoulder. "Tell no one. Show yourself to the priest and offer what Moses commanded."

I looked at him. How ironic that this man, not a ruler, would tell me, a Chief Pharisee, to follow the Law, to be declared "clean."

I entered the Temple that day, the first time in years. I didn't have to yell like a leper through the streets of my city, "Unclean. Unclean." I boldly walked up the stairs of the Temple, where the priest declared, "You are clean."

I returned to my own house, and I was called back to my position in the Temple.

My son became a follower of this Man. He claimed He was the one who would throw off the Roman rule from off our backs.

On one of Judas's visits home, he spoke of this Man's teachings. "He doesn't prepare armies, nor stir up the people. He talks of giving to the poor and loving your enemy."

I looked at Judas in pity. I squeezed his shoulder and felt him cringe. How could he be deceived? "You believe Him? He is only finding out who is true to Him before He shares His real plan. Stay with Him and tell me when He does."

Judas fidgeted, trying to back away from my touch. "He deceives the people well. I, too, am almost deceived."

I shook my head. "Do not be sucked into His kindness. He heals to draw a following. Then He will use it against Rome to overthrow its power. Keep me informed."

He nodded, hesitant to leave.

"What is it?"

"His disciples . . . they're crude fishermen. They don't even wash their hands when they eat bread."

I shook my head. "Yet He knows the Law?"

He nodded. "He speaks with authority."

"I will check into this. He must follow the Law, or He is not the one we want to deliver us from Rome. He will be like a foreigner imposing His rules on us."

I was tired of Rome demanding more taxes. I wearied of soldiers filling my city's streets. I hated Herod for bringing foreigners to rule in my Temple. I had heard enough of this Jesus, Who had a following that could overthrow the Roman Empire yet didn't lead us to freedom.

Judas nodded and slipped out the back gate.

I went to hear this Man and shook my head when I saw His disciples eating with unclean hands. Judas had been right. They were unclean. I approached Jesus, to instruct Him in the Law. "Why don't your disciples wash their hands when they eat?"

Several people in the group stood as I approached. They knew my position among the Pharisees. Jesus remained sitting, ignored my question, and asked His own. "Why do you transgress the commandment of God for the sake of your tradition? God said, 'Honor your father and mother,' and 'he who speaks evil of father or mother is to be put to death.' But you say, 'Whoever says to his father or mother, "whatever I have that would help you has been given to God" does not need to honor his father or his mother.' And by this you invalidated the word of God for the sake of your tradition. You hypocrites, rightly did Isaiah prophesy of you: 'This people honors Me with their lips, but their heart is far away from me. In vain they worship Me, teaching as doctrines the precepts of men.'"

I stepped back, surprised at His words. He *did* know the Law, but He twisted it to fit what He wanted it to say. I couldn't answer Him. Even as I considered, He turned to the crowd. "It's not what enters into the mouth that defiles the man, but what comes out of the mouth; this defiles the man."

I clenched my fists at my sides as my face flushed in anger. I caught Judas's eye.

He approached Jesus and whispered, "You've offended the Pharisees by Your words."

Jesus looked directly at me. "He is blind, leading the blind. Both will fall into a pit."

He made me look like a fool! How dare he accuse me of going astray! He judges me? Wasn't I the leader who pronounced clean or unclean for Temple worship? I looked at the crowds. They believed His words. I swallowed my anger. Another time I would respond, but I would remember this disgrace.

As I performed my duties at the Temple, Jesus's words lingered in my mind. I couldn't sleep. This Jesus had humiliated me before peasants! I must show them that He had deceived them. I started following Him, just so I could humiliate Him. I yelled from the back of the crowd, "Show us a sign from heaven."

Jesus nodded. "When it is evening, you say, 'It will be fair weather, for the sky is red.' And in the morning, 'There will be a storm today, for the sky is red and threatening.' How is it you can discern the sky, but cannot discern the times? An evil and adulterous generation seeks after a sign. And no sign will be given except the sign of Jonah." Then He walked away.

I had been dismissed. How dare He call me evil!

This was clearly not the Man we should follow. He would not work with the holy men of God. The scribes, Pharisees, even the Sadducees must unite to eliminate His power, crush His influence, and scatter His following. His insults against us were public . . . but we could not eliminate Him publicly. The people followed Him. He acted peacefully, but He stirred up the people with His words against the Temple and us. If we caused a riot, we would be put in Roman jails. And our own power would be crushed.

I cursed when I learned He had gone to Jerusalem and whipped our moneychangers and those who sold goods for the work of the Temple. We received a high percentage of their profits. He dared to enters our sanctuary and tells us how to worship God? He was definitely not the kind of man we wanted to overthrow Rome. He must be eliminated.

I called a meeting of all of the scribes, Pharisees, and Sadducees. We would plan how to get rid of Him discreetly.

I heard Judas slip into the house. "What is it?"

He seemed preoccupied. "He knows of your plans . . . to deliver Him to the Roman courts."

I paced. "How could he know? Did you let something slip?"

Judas shook his head, but backing away from me. "I said nothing, but He knew everything."

"What else did He say?"

Judas swallowed. "The Jerusalem chief priests and elders asked him by what authority He preached."

"Good question. What did He say?"

Judas shook his head. "He asked them by whose authority John baptized."

I considered. If they said from men, then the people would discount their words; but if they said of God, then He would ask, "Why didn't you believe him?"

"What did they say?"

Judas said, "They didn't know."

My shoulders slumped. He had outsmarted them again. "Did He answer their question then?"

Judas shrugged. "He said, 'Neither will I answer you by what authority I do these things.'"

I paced before the window. There must be some way to trip Him in His words. To show the people He is not who He claims to be. He undermined our authority and brought uncleanness to my soul.

Judas continued. "He pronounced woes on all the leaders of the Temple."

I turned from the window.

Judas seemed to find pleasure in sharing the Man's words. "He called you unclean. Clean on the outside, like a cup, but full of robbery and self-indulgence on the inside. He even called you whitewashed tombs . . . beautiful on the outside, but full of dead men's bones and uncleanness." Judas smirked.

I felt the blood rush to my face. My own son laughed at me, siding with this Man who destroyed our traditions. I moved quickly across the room and struck him across the face.

His smile disappeared. "I find His words true."

I stood face to face with Judas. "You don't know what clean is. You don't even bother to keep yourself pure for God."

Judas laughed now. "And you do? I saw who left your chamber before I entered . . . and it wasn't mother. What happened to the girl down the street . . . what was her name?"

"I don't know what you're talking about."

Judas shrugged. "Are you sure all the leprosy is gone?" He laughed. "Whitewashed tombs . . . what a good picture."

I raised my hand to smack him again, but stopped. In the light of the sunbeam from the window, my hand appeared white. I panicked and hid my hand in my robe. Who was unclean? It was just a recurring trick of my mind. I was fine.

I adjusted my thoughts to what we had been talking about. I needed Judas to help stop this Man. I clenched my fist in my robe's pocket and turned my back on him, looking out the window. I breathed deeply.

Judas turned to leave.

I wasn't done with him. "Caiaphas meets with the chief priests and elders."

"Caiaphas?"

I nodded. "We cannot seize Him in public. We would have a riot. We must find another way."

"Especially not during the festival." Judas added. "Have us for dinner. There would be no crowds, and I grow tired of sleeping in different houses every night."

I smiled, the first time since he entered. "What a good idea. Bring Him here."

I planned for His visit. I would show Him my wisdom and my place before God. I would also find out how He had come to know our plans. Maybe this would be the time to take Him.

When He came, bringing his disciples with him, Judas seemed ill at ease.

I drew him aside. "What is it?"

"What plans do you have?"

I shook my head. "This is not the place to discuss our plans."

He motioned me to the other room and whispered, "He told us He would be crucified."

"Crucified . . . how would He know that?"

"He told us."

I shook my head, looking through the doorway at Jesus as He reclined at my table. I had just come from a secret meeting of priests and elders. Caiaphas, the high priest, had plotted to seize Jesus and kill Him. I had told Judas nothing. I, too, was disturbed. I must be careful what I said. Someone was leaking information. Tonight would not work for taking Him. "We must find out how He knows."

Judas turned back to the table.

I grabbed his arm. "You are still with us. Aren't you?" I stared at him.

He held my gaze.

He twitched beneath my grasp. "Crucify Him? Father. Is that how you get rid of someone you can't answer? His truth makes me question what you taught me."

I swallowed the anger rising in my throat. "You question me?"

He laughed then. "Isn't that what you taught? We should not honor our fathers, but give to the Temple? I don't honor you, but neither will I give to the Temple. Because it only ends in your hands." He laughed, taunting me.

I glanced through the doorway, clenching my jaws.

Who had come to my house? Was that the woman from down the street? My hand stopped squeezing his arm.

Judas followed my gaze. "Seems like Jesus is not only stealing your prestige as a Temple leader but also taking your entertainment from your chamber."

I smacked him. The noise echoed in the hallway. I glanced quickly to see if the guests had noticed. "We will speak later."

Judas stood confident. "I look forward to it."

I followed Judas as we returned to the banquet room. I felt even more ill than before.

The woman, who had entered, was kneeling at Jesus's feet where He reclined, eating the grapes while they waited for the meal to start. She had started to weep. Her tears fell on His feet. Seeing nothing to wipe her tears from His feet, she loosened her braid of hair and used it to dry her tears.

I approached the table, knowing what kind of a woman she was. Hadn't she frequented my chamber before this Jesus had come? She had been unwilling once Jesus had become popular. Judas's words still churned within me. Hadn't Jesus taken both my authority and my chosen entertainment?

I made myself comfortable on the cushions and grabbed some grapes before speaking. I motioned toward Jesus's feet, in a gesture of disgust. "If you knew what kind of woman that is, you wouldn't allow her to touch you."

"Simon," Jesus paused to drink from his vessel. His tone sounded as if He considered me a wayward child. "Simon. You invited me to your house, yet when I entered, you didn't greet me with a kiss. This woman has not stopped kissing my feet. When I came into your house, you didn't wash my feet. She hasn't stopped washing my feet with her hair. You have offered me only a token of hospitality, but she has given me her heart."

While Jesus spoke, she took from her tunic's pocket a vial of perfume. She opened it, filling the air with its fragrance. The odor of unwashed bodies was replaced with its strong, sweet smell.

I watched, unable to eat, as she poured the entire contents over Jesus's head.

Judas leaned in beside Jesus, whispering loudly, "Why did she waste this perfume? She could have sold it for three hundred denarii and given the money to the poor."

Jesus's tone grew stern. "Leave her alone. You'll always have the poor with you. You won't always have Me. She has anointed my body for burial."

I coughed, choking on the fig I chewed.

He spoke of his burial. Did He know it was soon?

I wanted this Man out of my house. He had rebuked my lack of hospitality, making me feel unclean. He had defended this sinner, while condemning me!

His presence unsettled me, not only because He knew our plans, but mostly because He exposed my uncleanness.

I concealed my rage, but I hurried the meal to a close.

As He and His disciples left, Judas whispered to me, "When do the scribes meet again?"

Could I trust him? I studied him, finally telling where and when we would meet.

When Judas showed up at our meeting, I was troubled. Had I misplaced my trust? All discussion stopped as he stood before the chief priest. His voice was strong, confident. "I'll turn him over to you."

I felt a surge of relief and pride. This was my son. He would defend my honor. He would safeguard my position. I caught his eye and smiled.

The council agreed to pay him thirty pieces of silver and dismissed him.

As I left the meeting, I felt elated. This Man, who could see into my very heart, would be gone. This Man, who challenged my authority, questioned my cleanness, and misinterpreted our traditions and Law would be removed. I whistled as I made my way home.

The elation didn't last long. It was replaced by a growing unease. As we ate the Passover dinner at my house, the atmosphere seemed oppressive. I struggled to choke down the bitter herbs. The egg tasted of sand. The horseradish magnified my thirst. But when I finally drank from the wine, it soured my mouth and unsettled my insides.

When Judas interrupted my meal, I almost felt relieved.

"We have him!"

I listened as he explained where Jesus was. I sent servants to the Roman guard with instructions for taking this insurrectionist. Then I sent for the priests, scribes, and rulers to meet at the Temple.

The night was dark, without a moon to light my way. I tripped over a root in the pathway in my hurry to arrive. Tonight was the night our power would return. The scribes, Pharisees, and Sadducees waited in the darkening room to see if Judas would be successful.

I looked around the room. Even though shadows covered the faces of the men, they had pulled their head coverings low over their foreheads, as if they didn't want to be recognized. No one spoke. The waiting taxed us all.

The one candle on the table in front of the chief scribe was the only light.

I replayed all the questions Jesus had asked that I couldn't answer. How could our traditions not be right? Were they really contrary to the Law? I shook my head, fighting the doubts that seeped into the darkness and gripped me. I'm the man given God's authority to interpret the Law. Hadn't I studied it for years? Doubts seeped into the darkness and gripped me. I shook my head. Now wasn't the time to question what we were doing.

I was so preoccupied with my thoughts that when the candle sputtered, and flickered, I jumped.

Doubts crept in unbidden. I had been a leper, cleansed by Jesus's very hand. Jesus had called us clean on the outside, blemished on the inside. I crossed my arms and leaned against the wall. I could sense the dead man's bones He had spoken of. I could see the white of my leprous hand creeping into my heart and choking it. I shivered and shifted in my chair as I tried to control my thoughts. I was clean. I looked at the candle as it sputtered and went out.

We sat in the darkness. No one rose to light another.

The silence was broken by footsteps running in the passageway.

There was a shifting of chairs around me, and someone suddenly stood and relit the candle.

Judas appeared, panting at the doorway. "The deed is done."

I breathed deeply, and realized I had unconsciously been holding my breath.

The light wasn't strong enough to see Judas.

Someone finally took a candle from the scone in the hallway and brought it into the room. Even with the added light, the room seemed dark, stifling. The air close.

Judas looked anxious. "Where's the silver?"

The leader of the Sadducees slowly stood from his chair and opened the money chest. He dug through its contents, counting out thirty pieces in a pile. Each piece clanked on the table.

When he finished, Judas gathered them into his purse and pulled the drawstring tightly, securing the purse in the folds of his cloak. He walked to the doorway. Before leaving, he scanned the room until he found me. He nodded, then left.

No one spoke. The deed was done.

I should have felt relief; instead I felt a foreboding, a pressure on my heart that evil had replaced any cleanness I might have had. I scowled. I couldn't let His words change my mind now. I wouldn't go back to before He had come. I sighed, then looked around, for it echoed in the silent room. If I went back to before He had come, I'd still be a leper. I'd still be unclean. I shook my head. My thoughts wouldn't rest. Being unclean as a leper seemed mild compared to what I felt now.

When a chair scraped on the marble floor, I jumped. The chief scribe stood, calling us to move to the courtroom. We would try this Man who questioned our authority, who caused my insides to be feel unclean. We would remove Him and destroy these doubts.

I followed the others to the courtroom.

No execution trial could be held before morning sacrifices. That was the Law. Our minds must be clear. I looked for the sun. It wouldn't rise for many hours. No one reminded us of the Law we were breaking. We took our seats without protest. How could I shout so loudly for us to obey the Law when my own heart desired to destroy it?

I felt the evil of what we were doing. I studied my hands, expecting them to be white again. Could leprosy come back? I rubbed my hands on my tunic and shifted in my chair.

Roman soldiers brought Jesus into the room. His hands were bound behind him. But His hands were not what I feared, those Hands that had healed me of my leprosy. I feared His words. What would He say? He stood before us, looking at each one of us.

I felt as if I were on trial, not He. Why did I feel such uncleanness in His presence? I pulled my head covering further over my head and lowered my eyes. I couldn't watch this Man stand before these witnesses.

No one defended His cause: another Law we didn't obey. If we waited until morning, some of our own—Nicodemus, for one—would defend Him. We couldn't have that. The false witnesses we had prepared came forward to tell of His blasphemy. As they accused Him, His words pierced my heart, and I felt they were true. Could He be the Son of God?

We could execute someone according to our Law. For example, the woman we had caught in adultery, we could stone. But we wanted Jesus to be executed by the Romans, so the Jews would not riot against us. We must have a cause great enough for the Romans to execute Him.

Our Law didn't allow a death sentence to be given the day before a Feast or Sabbath. This was the day before the Passover. Our Law also required a two-day waiting period before any death penalty, to give time for consideration. But this rushed, secret trial in the middle of the night was necessary to keep the wrong witnesses showing up in favor of Him.

I swallowed the bile that rose in my throat at our disregard of our own Law. I watched Jesus's retreating back, as He was taken to Pilate for a Roman trial.

We changed the charges for the Roman court, to make them more convincing. He was a traitor to Rome, claiming to usurp the emperor.

The bones of the dead man Jesus had described seemed to be clawing at me. I shivered, but I didn't stop the proceedings.

When the trial went back and forth, between our group and Pilate, then even to Herod, I couldn't hold my dinner. I left to walk in the coolness of the garden behind the Temple. My hands shook as I studied them again for any white spot of leprosy.

I remembered that cleanness I had felt when Jesus had healed my leprosy. I had felt whole.

But now that feeling of wholeness, of purity, of cleanness was gone. Instead, I felt a rottenness gnawing at my insides, eating at my bones.

When I arrived at my chamber, I pushed my head covering off my head and rubbed my hands through my hair. Anguish grabbed my soul and sucked it dry, squeezing it until I couldn't breathe. Perhaps an hour or two of sleep before the day began would settle my nerves.

I turned toward my bed, and was surprised to see Judas on it.

He arose quickly when I saw him.

I tried to conceal my exhaustion and anguish. One glance at him told me I didn't need to.

He fell at my feet. The coins in his hand spilling out on the floor with a clattering that unnerved me.

I could barely understand him, as he wept at my feet, "I can't take these."

His prostrate form reminded me of my own weakness. He was grovelling on the ground like I had done when I was a leper. "Who am I to accept this money?" I spat at him. "Return it to the counsel who gave it to you!"

He raised his head. Tears had streaked his face. He pulled his hair in an effort to still his inward unrest.

I stepped back, unwilling to be made unclean by his wrongdoing. Without saying another word, I turned my back on him and stalked to my balcony, shutting the doors behind me. I wanted peace, cleanness, the purity of the Law.

I laughed out loud. I wanted the Law? I had broken the Law all night. I only wanted my own rules, my own traditions, my own way . . . And I had gotten it, but at what cost?

Later that day, after the sun had risen, when the chief priests met again, Judas appeared before them. I hardly recognized him. His eyes had a haunted look, like he had been sucked into the spirit world and only escaped with his body. His cloak was torn, his arms limp at his sides.

The chief priest demanded. "What do you want?"

His voice was hoarse, and it pained me to hear him. "I have sinned by betraying innocent blood."

"What is that to us?"

Judas threw the coins on the floor at their feet. They rolled and clanked. Before they stopped rolling, he was gone.

One Pharisee, not willing to see any money wasted, gathered them up off the floor.

I nearly stomped on his hand when he reached under my robe to take one that had rolled there. He placed them carefully on the table, where the night before the high priest had counted them out so carefully and Judas had taken them so willingly. What had a night wrought!

The High Priest coughed after seeing the coins. "It's not lawful to return them into the Temple treasury, since it's the price of blood."

I almost choked. We are concerned about what the Law says now? After disregarding it all night!

I listened in shock as they decided to buy the Potter's Field. It was a field unworthy of anything: full of rocks, boulders, and snakes. They bought it for a burial place for strangers. I nearly choked on the bile that remained in my throat from the night's activities.

Was this the group of men I had fought so hard to be like? Is this what we had become? A group that used the Law to gain power, money, and position, but did not use the Law to cleanse our own hearts?

I was called back to the trial. I entered the court, head down, unable to listen to the proceedings. What if Jesus was right? Would I ever feel the healing of cleanness on the inside?

We moved to where Pilate would stand on his balcony and announce his verdict.

Pilate asked, "What has He done?"

I stood with the mob of my peers, yelling, "Crucify Him. Crucify Him."

I remember Pilate's confusion. "I find no fault with Him."

Jesus's words pierced me. Whitewashed tombs. Whitewashed tombs. Nothing but dead man's bones. Bones. Bones. I screamed with the crowd. "Crucify Him." Could my screams cover my uncleanness? If He were gone, would my cleanness return? He made me feel unworthy.

We did crucify Him. Well, the Roman soldiers did. But I felt I hung Him on that cross.

Killing Him did not give me peace. I felt the guilt of what we had done. How could I now uphold the Law?

All of us scribes and rulers huddled in our court room after the trial and His death. What should we do now? We had not given any thought to that.

Joseph approached us for Jesus's body.

We hadn't considered this problem. Joseph was a wealthy man who gave much to the Temple and our purses. Would he stop if he knew our part in the Man's death?

We allowed Joseph to take the body. That would eliminate our problem. Everything would be forgotten. Life would go back to normal.

But guilt weighed heavy on my chest.

Someone suggested placing a guard at the tomb. Who knew what his followers would do with His body? We all thought it was a good idea.

I returned home, exhausted. The Passover night had turned into a nightmare.

We had accomplished what we wanted.

He was dead.

I laid down, trying to sleep, even though it was still day. All I managed to do was relive the irony of this Man's unjust trial. I heard a servant enter. "What is it?"

He bowed. "News has come of Judas."

"What of him?"

"He has hung himself."

I nodded. I could feel my uncleanness press on my heart. Judas had felt that same weight. I had seen it in his eyes when he begged me to take the coins. Did he think I could redo history? Change what wrong we had done? Judas was a coward. He died, trying to escape the guilt.

Couldn't I even raise a man who could stand up to the decisions he made? I didn't weep for the child I lost, I wept for the son I never loved. I wept for the Law I didn't understand. I wept for the cost of my decision.

What could I do now?

A thunderstorm at midafternoon, darkness like the deepest pit, made my skin crawl. I rubbed my hands to reassure myself that the leprosy hadn't returned. But how to rub the dead man's bones from the inside of my heart?

I dragged myself to the Temple on the Sabbath. It was time for evening sacrifices. I numbly partook of the lamb that was slain for the sins of the people.

Looking back now, I know the Law was made to show me my sin. Sacrifices pointed us to the Savior Who would die for our sins.

When this Man rose from the dead, I went to hear Him again. He spoke of victory over death, sin, and the grave. Could He make me clean . . . not just my skin, but inside and out? Could He take away the dead man's bones that haunted me?

He could, and He did.

Some days now, I stand on the mountainside and look over the Potter's Field. I weep over the son I never thought was good enough. Now I see I wasn't good enough to show him God. I see a woman who kissed the feet of her Savior because He had given her worth, not because of what she did, but because of Whose she was. I see graves of strangers buried at my feet, but not forever.

I see hope. Hope of being washed clean by the blood of the Lamb.

The Man I killed spilled His blood to wash my uncleanness away. I don't understand it. But I know it is so. I am clean, inside and out.

I am still known as Simon the Leper, even though no spot of white can be seen on my skin.

I still teach the Law, but not all the traditions that man has added.

I still strive to be clean. But I know it's not through my own efforts I'm made or even kept clean. It's only through the work of that Man I nailed to the cross.

I am Marinus, the Centurion

———— ❧ ————

W E HAD ARRIVED tired, ready to make camp outside Jerusalem's walls. Instead, we were called to still an uprising.

These insurrectionists were all the same. They thought if they murdered, they could gain enough of a following to overthrow Rome. What fools! We had enough strength and troops to quell any uprising in the world.

I gathered my hundred men to calm whatever unrest the Jews had stirred up in the city of Jerusalem.

When we reached the back alleys, the crowd parted before me, so I could see the body that lay in middle of the street. I turned him over with my foot. He had been stabbed several times. Didn't even know what hit him.

I glanced around. The crowd shrank from my gaze, opening a view to a man restrained by three other men against a wall of the house. He continued to fight, spewing out his hatred for Rome and its power, calling his people to resist and fight back.

I cracked my rod over his back to silence him. No one spoke against Rome in my presence.

He cowered from me, still glaring his hatred. My men restrained him and bound his arms behind his back.

I surveyed the crowd. "Any others involved in this?"

They only stared back at me, dumb and unresponsive.

I motioned to my sergeant to direct the removal of this vermin. His trial wouldn't be long in coming. Rome removed rebels quickly. She raised them on crosses where all could see the results of their rebellion.

Crucifixion.

I thrived on Rome's control over all people. Aligning myself with Rome and joining the ranks of her vast army had given me power. But crucifixion was gruesome. No other torture could change a man so. I had to remind myself they were insurrectionists when I watched them die.

I shook my head and looked at my men now. They were disciplined. Our legion, 60 centurions with a hundred men each, had swelled into the city.

The Jews were having some feast day, and the city was packed with travelers who had come to celebrate.

Pilate had anticipated problems and had requested more troops.

We had come from the north, Sidon. The distance, although long, had been covered in just seven days. My men could march twenty-two Roman miles in five hours, while carrying our weapons and campsite supplies. This was expected of the army; demanded by me. We represented the power of Rome. We displayed her strength.

Many joined the army for a twenty-five-year commitment, hoping to rise in the ranks, at least to reach my rank; it offered a comfortable salary. Their current, meager pay would be forgotten, and their virtue and bravery would be acknowledged.

I wiped my forehead before putting my helmet back on. Already I missed the breezes, blowing from the Great Sea. I hoped this city would not hold me too long. The city was hot, unlike the sea coast we had left behind. The dullness of this commission wearied me. My men were already bored with what this small city offered.

I was assigned to the Temple of the Jews. I was supposed to pacify the religious leaders and keep the people from unrest. Jews were more volatile than other people, especially about their religious days and their Temple.

I gathered my men and reported to the Temple to maintain order. We arrived to find another disturbance. Doves were flying through the air. Sheep were running loose.

I heard yelling from within the Temple.

I pushed my way up the crowded stairs to see the cause of the disturbance. Money clattered onto the marble floor. More animals ran through my legs to escape the crowded entryway and run down the street.

When I reached the front of the crowd, I saw tables overturned. A Man upended another table where the merchants were exchanging their Hebrew shekels for Roman currency.

One merchant grabbed his money, guarding it against his chest, before his table's contents were dumped on the floor. His animals scattered.

The Man who had overturned the tables glared at the merchants. "My house shall be called a house of prayer for all the nations! But you . . . " He stepped toward the merchants cowering against the wall behind where their tables had once protected them. He pointed at them. "You have made it a robbers' den."

I surveyed the room. Who was at fault? Sounded like the mer-chants were the thieves and they had just been caught in their crime.

The religious leaders had gathered to see the commotion, watching from the doorway of the inner chamber of the Temple. They showed no sign of stopping this Man, though they were clearly angry. Did He hold some power over them?

What should I do?

Time stopped as all watched what this one Man would do.

He waited.

He watched the merchants.

Finally, as if by an invisible thread of conscience, the merchants began leaving with bowed heads. They left all their stock and walked down the Temple stairs. Some hesitantly grabbed money from the floor before retreating behind the others.

The people parted, making a path for them.

I caught my breath, not even knowing I had held it. What had transpired here? What power did this Man possess over even the religious rulers? They didn't looked pleased. Their neck veins bulged. Their faces were red. They would have exploded, if the people had not been there.

Now, they covered their uneasiness by directing their servants to clean up the mess.

They set up tables and picked up the forgotten money.

Their Temple must be made clean.

I nodded, secretly pleased with the tension. I enjoyed a good fight. Perhaps this stay in Jerusalem would not be too dull after all.

The highest leader looked at me, hatred in his gaze. My men's presence in their "holy" Temple was an outrage to them.

I stared him down. Rome's power was greater than the power of a lowly priest. After another look around to assure myself we weren't needed. I directed my men outside the Temple again.

Nothing more was required of us. There had been no violence; merely a Temple cleaning. I smiled inwardly. I could follow a Man like that.

Much of the crowd had followed the Man as He left the Temple. I would have myself, if I could have. He possessed a power by His very words that drew me.

The week progressed. Our presence curbed any disturbances.

I watched for the Man who had made such a commotion in the Temple, commanding the respect of the people, and the fear of their leaders. But I didn't see Him again. I was disappointed.

The Jews' Passover approached. I had ordered my men to their respective posts. They were not to be caught leaning against any wall, but to stand straight and stare ahead, as they monitored the streets. Their discipline would reflect the Rome they served. A passer-by wouldn't even notice them standing there, they stood so still. But if a disturbance occurred, they'd be ready.

Another quiet night.

Yet the quiet seemed deceptive. I sensed a stirring underneath the quietness that left me anxious.

I stood with a few other centurions when a messenger arrived.

He stood panting before our group. "The leaders of the Temple request your help."

I was immediately alert. The Jews never asked for our help. Their disdain for us was clear. Was this a trap?

He paused, trying to catch his breath. "They are requesting a cohort to bring in an insurgent. Meet at the Temple to be directed to the man."

We moved as one, calling our men to march. At the Temple courtyard, big enough for our six groups of a hundred men to assemble, I saw no disturbance.

No one was there.

Then I noticed a man pushing his way through the rows of soldiers to get to the Temple.

The messenger, who still stood near me, answered my unspoken question. "He's the one the Temple leaders are waiting for."

I nodded.

We waited a few minutes before the man returned and with him several servants, probably sent from the leaders inside.

He directed us, "Follow me. We will be capturing a dangerous man, Jesus the Nazarene. I will show you who He is."

I fell in line with the others. My men in front held torches, for darkness had already fallen. I wondered what kind of rebel group would require six hundred men to stop their activities.

The messenger led us into an olive grove.

I checked the dagger on my right side, then realigned my sword on the left.

As the torch light penetrated the darkness, the silhouette of a group came into focus. The torch's light reflected off their faces, and it took some time for my eyes to focus with the light.

Then I saw the face of the Man from the Temple before us. So this was how the religious leaders would get even. I gave no outward sign, but swallowed my disgust for their lack of courage.

The Man stood quietly in front of a mere handful of unarmed followers.

He would cause an uprising with these?

I glanced around the shadows for more. Had we walked into a trap?

Our informant approached the Man with confidence. "Rabbi."

The Man didn't appear surprised. "Friend, do what you have come for."

The betrayer, for I saw him for who he was, stepped forward and kissed the Man. Then he stepped back, expecting our immediate response.

The Man shook his head. "Judas, you betray the Son of Man with a kiss?" He turned then and acknowledged our presence. "Whom do you seek?"

I answered. "Jesus, the Nazarene."

He stood tall. "I Am He."

My knees suddenly buckled under me. Not by my own will . . . His words held the power of God. Part of me was confused as I bowed before this Man Who was not even a Roman ruler. And yet there was something about Him that made me want Him as my supreme King. I felt I would be happy to submit to Him. I bowed my head to the ground, forgetting what we had come here for.

He again asked, "Whom do you seek?"

I answered again, but this time I didn't speak with power nor authority. I spoke from the ground. "Jesus the Nazarene."

"I told you I Am He."

Who was this Man, that our entire Roman cohort had fallen before Him?

I stood then, hearing around me the others' armor clank as they also rose to their feet.

His followers stepped to His side. "Lord, shall we strike them with the sword?"

"No."

But even as He spoke, one of His followers swung with his sword. What an inexperienced swing! With his wild swing, he managed to cut off the ear of a servant standing by the informer. I almost laughed out loud. This one hoped to defend the Man!

Before any could respond, this Man reached out, touched the bleeding ear, and healed it. He rebuked His follower, "Put away your sword."

I stepped forward to grab His follower.

He faced me. "I told you, I Am He; so if you seek Me, let these go their way. All those who take up the sword shall perish by the sword. Don't you know I could appeal to My Father, and He would send more than twelve legions of angels to My aid?"

Twelve legions of angels! We had brought 600 men, and we could not even stand before His words. What would He do with twelve legions—5,000 foot soldiers plus cavalrymen?

I studied the sky, even though there was no moon. Were there angels waiting to destroy us? What god could save us then?

Who was this Man?

He was not finished. "The Scriptures must be fulfilled. Should I not drink the cup which My Father has given Me?"

This was no normal insurrectionist, who fought until we proved our superior might. This Man owned all power, yet submitted to us. I didn't understand.

I shook my head, trying to regain my usual air of command, even as I obeyed His command to let His follower go.

For the first time since our approach, He spoke to the chief rulers' servants, "You come with swords as you would against a robber? I stood before you daily in the Temple, yet you didn't touch Me. But this is your hour of darkness."

I stepped forward now, willing myself to do my duty and seize Him. Yet even in this, I sensed my impotence. I didn't take this Man, He gave Himself to me. His power could crush any Roman legion that approached Him. Hadn't He brought our entire cohort to our knees by His spoken word?

He allowed us to bind His hands behind His back. I wondered what good that would do if He decided to speak His words of power again. He turned away from His disciples.

We led Him to the Temple court room where their chief priests and rulers had gathered.

I listened as they set up court, struggling to maintain my stoic soldier posture.

They were jealous of His power.

I wanted to tell them, the sway He held over the common people was something no man could have for himself. It was a supernatural power, that no man could take for his own.

There was a strength The Man seemed in contrast to their presence.

A new group of soldiers came to take our shift.

I wanted to stay. I wanted to know what they would do to this Man.

Instead, I returned to camp with my soldiers. They slept, but sleep didn't come for me. Who was this Man Who could cause an entire army to fall before Him with only His words?

The Man's words rang through my mind all night, "Those who live by the sword will die by the sword." Wasn't that what I wanted? To die in battle, fighting for Rome?

When the sun rose, my shift came back on duty, and I still had no answer to my questions. Rome had been my source of power since I had begun this soldier's life. I had dreamed of power. With that as my goal, I had risen in the soldiers' ranks, becoming the leader that I now was.

I inspected my men as they stood at attention; then commanded them to march to Pilate's palace, where we were to keep order during the morning watch. There was a gathering there by the time we arrived. We stood back, watching, ready to interfere if the crowd became a mob.

Pilate stood on his balcony with the Man beside him. So the Jewish rulers had shuffled Him to Pilate. How had they managed that?

Pilate raised his arms to quiet the crowd. "You brought this Man as one who incites rebellion. I find no fault in Him. Nor has Herod, for he sent Him back to me. He's done nothing deserving death. I will punish Him and release Him."

I swayed on my feet as I began to understand the Jews' plan. They were trying to have the Romans blamed for this Man's death. I could see through their plan now. They didn't want their own people to rise up against them. If they could blame the Romans for His death, they even had a chance to incite the people to revolt against Rome. It was a clever plan. However, they forgot that Rome, although hard, was just.

But even as I understood their plan, they cried, "Away with this Man."

I watched Pilate hesitate. He was a weak ruler, catering to the whims of these people.

Jesus swayed on his feet. It looked like the night shift soldiers had harassed Him. He was wearing a crown of thorns and a purple robe. His beard had been ripped off. If I hadn't brought the Man to the leaders the night before, I wouldn't have recognized Him.

Pilate pointed to Him. "I find no fault with this Man."

The rulers shouted, even louder, "Crucify Him!"

Pilate shook his head "Take Him yourselves and crucify Him, for I find no guilt in Him."

The rulers answered, "We have a Law, and by that Law He ought to die, because He made Himself out to be the Son of God."

Pilate turned pale. He swallowed and looked back at the Man. He commanded Jesus to be taken back inside.

The crowd waited, but not patiently. They were the same leaders who had been in the courtroom the night before. The night's activities had only heightened their hatred.

Pilate returned to his balcony. "I could release this Man."

The Jews accused, "If you release this Man, you're no friend of Caesar. Everyone who makes himself out to be a king opposes Caesar."

Pilate dropped his head.

They had cornered him.

Couldn't Pilate stand on the Man's innocence? I felt it. I knew it. But if Pilate didn't cater to the leaders, there would be a mob. His career would be over. He'd be replaced.

The leaders knew they had won. They chanted, "Away with Him. Crucify Him."

Pilate shook his head. "Shall I crucify your King?"

"We have no king but Caesar."

Pilate brought out another man. ""You will have to choose, then, between this Man or Barabbas!"

I recognized the man. He was the man we'd taken at the beginning of Surely the Jews would be forced to choose Barabbas' death. They wouldn't openly take the side of an anti-Rome fanatic.

Pilate was clearly desperate to release Jesus.

I could feel my heart willing to release Him, too.

But it seemed the rulers were beyond reason. They were driven by their jealousy and rage. And they had succeeded by now in stirring up the crowd. Mob control took over. Even those who had recently gathered to see what was happening began to echo the religious leaders. "Release Barabbas! Crucify Jesus!"

Pilate asked again. "Why? What has He done? Nothing that demands death."

The mob chanted as one.

I stood taller, watching for violence and an excuse to end this madness.

Pilate didn't want a mob. He wouldn't look good before Herod.

He released Barabbas, but washed his hands in front of the crowd, announcing, "I'm innocent of this Man's blood."

The leaders cried even louder, "His blood shall be on us and on our children."

I stood there, watching an innocent Man being condemned as a criminal. What could be done to stop this? I remembered His power when He stood before us. Surely, He wouldn't allow His own death, especially when it was unjust.

My stomach churned.

My country, Rome, under the rule of Pilate, had allowed this.

Where was justice? Couldn't Rome stand against these religious rulers?

Pilate wrote an inscription to be put on the cross: "Jesus, the Nazarene, the King of the Jews." He wrote it in Hebrew, Latin, and Greek.

The chief rulers corrected Pilate, "Don't write, 'The King of the Jews,' but that He claimed to be the king of the Jews."

Pilate shook his head. "What I have written stands."

I spread my men out among the crowd as the mob lined the streets, waiting for those to be crucified to walk toward Golgotha, the Place of the Skull.

When the convicts came, I gasped. The Man staggered, barely able to stand under the weight of His own cross. When He fell, one of the soldiers who kept the people back grabbed a man from the side to carry it for Him.

What had happened to this Man who had whipped the merchants from the Temple? As He passed me, I understood. A crown of thorns dug into his head, the blood blinding him. His back held no flesh. Pilate had punished him all right.

I hadn't been called on to punish Him; for that I was glad. My job was to control the mob. But what would a mob do in the face of such agony?

I had plenty of time to reflect that day, as I stood watching the crucifixion of the Man Who had captivated me. Having seen His power, I recognized the power of Rome for what it was . . . a power based on cruelty, putting others down, manipulating men by offering false hopes.

I gazed on this Man, His blood congealed on His face from the thorns, His beard been ripped from his face, His body scourged to the point many would have died from that alone. How long could He live?

The mid-morning sun was intense. I took my helmet off to wipe my forehead and replaced it again. I was not accustomed to this city's heat, even in spring.

I watched my own men gambling over His seamless tunic, woven as one piece. They had already divided his other garments into four portions and claimed them. I turned away. The soldiers were poor, barely making enough to eat, yet finding enjoyment at the foot of a cross that held a Man Who should not die.

I listened to the criminals crucified on either side of Him. One mocked His title, even as the chief priests did. "Are you the Christ? Save Yourself and me, too!"

Other spectators picked up the taunt. "He saved others; He can't save Himself. Let this Christ, this King of Israel, come down from the cross, so that we may see and believe."

The other criminal disagreed. "Don't you fear God? We suffer justly, getting what we deserve; but this Man has done nothing wrong." He paused before raising himself again to get a breath. "Jesus, remember me when You come into Your Kingdom."

The Man raised Himself to breathe, pushing against his feet that were spiked to the cross. As he lifted Himself, He was able to speak. "Today, you shall be with Me in Paradise."

My trust in Rome's power seemed ill-placed. If Rome did not hold true justice in her hand, where could I find hope? My strength and power seemed as nothing when I could not even save an innocent Man.

I watched His blood pool beneath Him on the cross.

Could He give me the same hope He had given the criminal at His side? How could He offer hope, even in His death? I did not understand.

The chief rulers and leaders mocked. "Bah. You were going to destroy the Temple and rebuild it in three days. Save Yourself and come down from the cross!" They turned to the people, trying to rile them, as if they had finally found power over Him. "If He trusts in God, let God rescue Him now, if He delights in Him; for He said, 'I am the Son of God.'"

The Man spoke, even though it cost Him great effort. "Father, forgive them. They don't know what they're doing."

Usually when we crucified people, I felt satisfaction. Rome had conquered another criminal. Rome had done justly. But with this Man . . . I shook my head. Rome had been unjustly. She had caved to the whims of a group of religious leaders, too cowardly to kill on their own. But they weren't the only ones. I had been in the Garden. I had laid hands on Him. I had brought Him to trial.

I remembered the feel of the dirt where I had fallen to my knees before Him. Had it only been last night? And yet I had gotten up, pushed aside my sense of awe for this Man, clung to my image as a Roman centurion, and arrested Him.

The sign above the cross seemed to mock me. Could this Man be the Son of God?

What had we done?

I lowered my head as the impact of His words hit me. He had just asked that I be forgiven.

And suddenly the sun grew dark. It was only noon. There had been no clouds moments before. The timing, just after this Man's words, made my heart grow cold.

Thunder rolled, echoing off the surrounding mountains. Lightning struck nearby. But no one ran for cover. They continued to watch this Man hang on the cross.

I squinted through the darkness, watching His labored breathing. All His weight rested on His feet. If He didn't raise himself up against the cross, He would suffocate. Every breath required this movement. Getting enough air to speak required greater effort.

I barely heard Him when He whispered. "I'm thirsty."

A vessel full of wine had been left there from another crucifixion. A follower grabbed a branch of hyssop and placed a cloth soaked with the wine on the end.

I could smell the rankness of it.

Another yelled, "Don't give it to him. See if He calls Elijah to save Him."

Ignoring their jeers, the follower placed the cloth to his Master's lips.

Jesus licked it, but when He had tasted it, He closed His mouth, and turned his head away, though the effort cost Him.

I licked my own lips, as if it would help Him with His thirst. Why wouldn't He accept a bit of pain reliever? Must He suffer all the agony of a common criminal?

His life lingered, though His breathing came more shallowly as His strength lessened. I had seen enough men die that I knew His life was leaving.

I tried to will Him to breathe again.

The other criminals seemed less stressed, but they hadn't been beaten as He had. He had bled so much even before He was put on the cross that it was a wonder He had lived long enough to be crucified.

He cried out again, this time in a loud voice that carried across the hillside, "It is finished." Then He bowed His head.

The Man, who held such power in His words, was dead.

My entire body felt empty. I had witnessed His power, but it had vanished before I could even understand it. I didn't know what to do with this loss.

The other criminals, hanging on either side of the Man, were still breathing. We would have to break their legs to speed their death. Then they would have no way to raise themselves up to breathe and would die of suffocation.

The Jews were adamant about their laws and had made it clear this job had to be finished before the sun set and their holy day began. One of the soldiers raised a metal rod to hit the first criminal's legs. The whack of the metal bar against his legs echoed loud over the hillside. The criminal crumbled, gasping for his last breath. The soldier moved to the other criminal on the other side of the Man, finishing his death.

When he came to the Man, the soldier paused, muttering, "He's dead already." He seemed surprised and disappointed.

I was not. I looked at the blood pooled at the bottom of His cross. I was exhausted, and I hadn't been through what He had.

"Wait." I demanded. I took the javelin from one of my men standing by and approached the Man on the cross. I pierced His side, reaching into His heart. When blood and water poured out, it was a sure sign that He was dead. His heart broken.

The blood and water ran down the javelin and I hurried to give it back to the man who stood beside me. I wiped His blood from my hands on my tunic.

I felt empty. Hopeless, I shook my head, willing myself to maintain control.

His followers had stayed the entire time, watching, crying. Even the women, who normally couldn't bear to watch such agony and torture.

I had no idea what time it was. It had been dark as a moonless night, until I had thrust the spear through Him. Then the sun had broken through the clouds. The angle of its rays told me evening had come.

When the beams shone through, I breathed deeply, as if the darkness had hindered my breathing.

I heard my own voice saying what I knew in my heart to be true. "Truly, this Man was the Son of God." I had witnessed His power. Now I understood it. But it was too late.

I led my men down the hill and felt an emptiness in our display of authority. Rome had no true power. She only took what she could. My insides were empty. I didn't understand this helplessness.

Pilate demanded that our legion stay in the city. He feared a mob.

I could have told him no mob could wreak any worse damage than had already been done.

Initially, I had wanted to leave this city; the heat, dirt and dullness making my skin crawl. But it was because I had to stay that I heard the Man's followers saying He had risen from the dead.

I sought out the Roman guard who had been assigned to watch His tomb. It had seemed to me a ridiculous request that we Romans guard a dead man's tomb. Until the body went missing.

The centurion on duty told me in private, under oath that I wouldn't speak a word, how two men in shining clothes had come and rolled the stone away. That same stone had required six strong Roman soldiers to put it in place. Another example of this Man's power . . . good thing He hadn't sent those legions of angels He had spoken of in the Garden.

At my silence, the centurion hesitated, clearly unwilling to tell me anymore. I told him how I had fallen on my face before the Man when we arrested Him. Then he seemed willing to share how the entire guard had fallen on their faces in terror; then fled.

He smirked a bit.

"What is it?" I demanded.

"The religious leaders paid all of us money to say that His disciples came by night and stole Him away, while we slept."

I laughed. "While you slept?" If they had slept on guard duty, they wouldn't be alive. "But what if Pilate should hear about your sleeping while on guard duty?"

He shrugged. "The Jews promised to keep us out of trouble."

I nodded. Any amount of money could control people. That's why Rome was so powerful. She controlled all money. I almost didn't hear the centurion continue.

"I'm going home. I have enough money to retire early from the Roman army and live like a king."

I gasped. "They gave you *that* much money?"

He laughed again. "But I don't think their plan will work; not with the Man walking around telling everyone that He's alive."

I went to see the tomb, now heavily guarded. Because of my uniform and status, I was allowed to enter the tomb.

It was indeed empty.

But not as if someone had stolen the body. It was as if His body had risen up out of the grave clothes and left them lying in His shape. Nobody stealing a body would want to unwrap it first.

I didn't touch the grave clothes.

They seemed too holy.

How could I know this Man, this God, this King, who accepted the agony of death on the cross, when He could have called a legion of angels?

I searched for His followers, hoping if I found them, I would find Him. I followed the crowd, almost running to Galilee.

He was there.

His followers worshipped Him. And rightly so.

Jesus spoke, "All authority has been given to Me in heaven and on earth. Go, and make disciples of all the nations. I am with you always, even to the end of the age."

I believed.

I knew He was the Son of God. He truly had all power. And He gave His authority to us.

I can say "us" now, because I follow Him too. I'm still a Roman soldier, but not seeking the power of Rome to overthrow all people. I am waiting for the Kingdom of My God and King, Jesus the Nazarene, whom I arrested, whom I watched as He surrendered His life, so that I could live by the power of His Father.

I don't crave power anymore. I have it. Not by conquering people, but by showing them the Savior Who willingly gave up His power so all can know Him.

I am Nicodemus

⚜

Iᴡɪʀsᴛ sᴀᴡ ᴛʜᴇ crowds gathered on the hillside around Jerusalem. Curious, I went to see. The people listened, not as if they were bored, like at the synagogue, but as if they were thirsty, soaking in as much as they could. The speaker told of a kingdom I could only dream of living in. He spoke of a life I had often longed for.

"Blessed are the poor in spirit, for theirs is the Kingdom of Heaven. Blessed are those who mourn, for they shall be comforted."

I drank in the gracious words.

He spoke of "fulfilling the Law." He pointed to me and some of the other Pharisees with me as He said, "I assure you that unless your righteousness surpasses that of the scribes and Pharisees, you will not enter the Kingdom of Heaven."

I knew the Law with its severity and structure. It made me feel sinful as if I'd never be really clean. But how could I be more righteous? How could I enter the Kingdom of Heaven? His words awakened a yearning in my heart to know more.

As a Pharisee, I had grown up studying the Law. I was part of the Sanhedrin, the Jewish ruling council. I was also a teacher of the Law.

But though I knew the Law, what I really wanted was to know God. How had Moses talked with God face to face? Why had God shown Himself then? Why had He not spoken to His people now for more than 400 years? What must we do to hear from God? What must I do?

When I returned to the Temple, I was excited to share with the council what I had heard. But before I could say a word, I saw Simon. He had been a chief priest years ago, but had gotten leprosy. "Simon!" I gasped, scanning him quickly for signs of leprosy.

He smiled. "I've been declared 'clean.'"

"How?"

"A Man called Jesus healed me."

It was the Man I had listened to; the One I had come to tell everyone about. Simon, too, had seen Him! Now we could tell the good news together.

But Simon looked troubled. "He allows the poor to be His followers. He attracts unlearned into His deception. He casts out demons because He is controlled by a demon."

Others joined in with their cautions about this Man. I stepped back from the group, confused. Why weren't the rulers pleased? Hadn't they had a chance to hear Him for themselves as I had?

They spilled more accusations, "The people give Him money, as if He could make them clean!"

"Some even worship Him, and He doesn't correct them."

"We've warned Him, but He won't listen to us. He thinks He's better than we are."

So they had heard the Man. They were jealous of Jesus!

I stepped from the room and looked toward the East Gate where I knew Jesus stood preaching. Was I wrong to be drawn by His words? I would keep my longing to myself until I knew more.

I wanted more. I was like a hungry man finally given a crumb of bread. It was not enough.

Every night for a week after that I woke in a pool of sweat, breathing raggedly. My unrighteousness seemed to press on me. It contrasted with this Man's purity. It seemed the more I listened to Him, the more I felt unworthy. Every night, I dreamt of slipping down a cliff with no bottom. With every night, I fell farther.

My wife rolled over. "Another dream?"

I caught my breath. "I reached for a hand, stretching for me. I was saved from the rocks below."

My wife, now fully awake, asked, "Why did you scream, 'Not you!'?"

I shuddered. "The council is jealous of Jesus. His following is great. He speaks with authority, even in the synagogues. . . . It was He Who saved me."

We sat in silence.

My wife finally spoke. "Go, speak to Him."

"Now?"

"Yes."

"But it's night."

"You need answers. You won't sleep until you have them."

My wife was right. My dreams hadn't been easy since I had heard His words. I must know more. But what would I ask Him?

I was surprised when I found him awake and alone. I stepped toward him from behind a tree. "Teacher." I didn't know what else to say, now that I had come.

Jesus wasn't surprised by my presence. He acted as if He'd been expecting me.

I didn't know how to ask my questions, "You come from God," I began. "No one can do these miracles unless God is with Him."

He looked deep into my eyes. "Unless a man is born again, he can't see the Kingdom of God."

His words puzzled me. I wanted to be part of this Kingdom of God, but I had no hope of being "born again." Was His Kingdom lost to me then? "How can an old man like me be born a second time?"

Jesus sat down by a well and motioned for me to sit. "Unless one is born of water and the Spirit, he can't enter the Kingdom of God."

I felt this Kingdom slipping from my grasp. What did He mean by being born of the Spirit?

Jesus tilted his head.

A breeze blew.

Feeling the chill against my cheek, I pulled my cloak tighter around me.

"Hear the wind blowing? Where does it come from?"

I shook my head. How could anyone know?

"That's how it is when the Spirit moves."

I hesitated, confused. I hated to show my ignorance. Wasn't I a ruler who instructed others about God?

But I thought of my wife. She would ask if my questions were answered. "How can these things be?" I asked.

Jesus responded as if He had heard my thoughts, "Are you a teacher of Israel, and yet you don't understand? If I tell you of earthly things and you don't believe, how can I tell you of heavenly things? The Son of Man has come from heaven. Just as Moses lifted up the serpent in the wilderness, so must the Son of Man be lifted up."

I knew this story story well. The Israelites in their journey to the Promised Land had complained. God had sent snakes among them. Anyone bitten would die within hours. That's how I felt. Like I was bitten and soon to die.

But Moses had interceded for the people, and God told him to lift up a bronze serpent on a cross. Those who looked to the serpent were spared. Who would intercede for me?

Jesus continued. "He that believes in the Son will have eternal life. For God so loved the world, that He gave His only begotten Son, that whoever believes in Him shall not perish, but have eternal life. For God didn't send His Son into the world to judge the world, but to save the world."

I saw His hand reaching toward me, just like in the dream, to save me from falling over the cliff. But this was a spiritual cliff.

Did He know how deeply the snake had bitten me? Did He realize how unclean I was? I knew the Law well enough to know I was guilty. I was unworthy.

At the same time, I knew He was pure and guiltless. He was worthy. He could save me. But how?

He broke into my thoughts. "The Light has come into the world. But men love the darkness rather than Light, because their deeds are evil."

Did He think I was evil, because I came at night? Was He telling me to leave and come back in the daytime? I looked down, not willing to leave without answers.

But then I thought of Simon. Even though he had been healed, he still didn't believe. Was Jesus warning me of the other rulers in the Temple?

Jesus looked at the moon, its glow making a path to His feet. "He who practices the truth comes to the Light, so that his deeds may be shown as coming from God."

I nodded. I could stand for what I believed, even when those around me wanted to stay in the darkness.

I would think about these things. He had given me answers I could hold on to, like the hand in my dream.

I left before the sun rose in the sky. But even though the sky was still dark, my heart glowed with a Light Jesus had put there. I was closer to meeting with God, just like Moses.

The next day in the Temple, My colleagues were grumbling about Jesus. Even though they didn't follow Him, they were consumed with what He said. That's all they would talk about.

I confronted them, "Why do you reject Jesus's words when He speaks truth?"

They didn't want to hear His words or the prophecies that He fulfilled.

Simon fought hardest. "How can the Messiah come out of Galilee? The Scriptures teach that Christ will come from David's descendants in the town of Bethlehem."

I didn't understand how someone could be healed from the dreaded disease of leprosy and still not consider Jesus the Messiah. Hadn't we all been waiting for Him? And now that He had come, why wouldn't they accept Him? "Listen to His teaching, Simon. No man has ever spoken like Him."

Simon spit. "You've been led astray like the masses. None of the Pharisees, besides you, have been deceived by Him."

A group had gathered.

I shook my head. "Our Law doesn't judge a man unless it first hears from him and knows what he is doing."

Another Pharisee asked, "Are you from Galilee, too?"

I swallowed. Being accused of coming from Galilee was the ultimate of insults. Galileans were unlearned, ignorant people. I felt my face flush as I thought of the light Jesus had told me to be.

Simon jabbed deeper. "Do the Scriptures tell of any prophet coming from Galilee?"

I shook my head. There was more to Jesus's background than living in Galilee, I felt sure. But I didn't understand it all myself. I walked away. I couldn't make them see. Nor would they change my mind.

I understood Jesus's words about being a light. I stuck out like a candle in the middle of a closed tomb. The darkness could easily swallow me if I dared to breath too deeply.

Friends, who had always respected my counsel, avoided me now, even ignoring my existence. I felt like an outcast.

Was I right? How could I understand spiritual things, when other leaders, better than I, couldn't seem to grasp them?

I clung to the words of Jesus about men choosing to stay in the darkness. Whatever the cost, I longed to know the Light.

One night, I returned to the Temple, long after the sun had gone down. I wanted to re-read a passage of Scripture that had come to my mind while Jesus had been preaching.

When I entered the Temple, I was surprised at how brightly lit it was. Many candles lit the hallway leading to the council room. Had I forgotten an important meeting? Why were they meeting at night?

I headed toward the council room.

Angry voices shouted, "He made a fool out of me! We must do something about Him!"

I slowed my steps. Were they speaking of Jesus?

They had questioned Him today about the greatest command, not sincerely, but trying to find fault with Him.

Jesus had silenced them with His answer.

When I stepped into the room, it suddenly became quiet. I felt I had trespassed. Wasn't I one of the chief rulers? I cleared my throat. "Did I forget a meeting?" Of course, I hadn't; no respectable meeting would be held during the night. Jesus's words about men loving darkness came back to my mind.

Several shifted in their seats, but no one answered. One by one they stood, acting as if they would leave. As if I would believe they had gathered by chance. They made me angry by their deceptiveness. They wanted me to leave. I stood there and waited until they left.

I was disturbed by this secret meeting. What were they planning?

As the days passed, the undercurrent of evil seemed so thick I could walk on it. I dreaded going to the Temple. I could talk to no one. They had only angry words, arguments, and hateful glares for me.

Instead, I spent more time following Jesus and searching what the Scriptures said.

He spoke about being His disciple. "If you continue in My Words, then you are truly disciples of Mine; and you will know the truth, and the truth will make you free."

Simon had come to stand beside me as I listened to Jesus.

Why did he associate with me in public, while avoiding me at the Temple? I held my breath, silently begging him not to start another argument with Jesus. Even though I believed Jesus's words, I felt sorry for my colleagues who continued daily to challenge Him. Didn't they realize their arguments would only show their need for Him?

But when I heard Simon lick his lips, I knew he would challenge Jesus again.

Simon called out, "We are Abraham's descendants and have never yet been enslaved to anyone; how is it that You say, 'You will become free'?"

Jesus stepped toward us. "Anyone who sins is a slave to sin. The slave doesn't remain in the house forever, but the son does."

I understood the feeling of slavery. The Law bound me. I labored to obey it, but it would never set me free. I longed for freedom.

"You may be Abraham's descendants, yet you seek to kill me, because My words have no place with you. I do things which My Father has shown Me, just like you do the things from your father."

Would they resort to killing? Was that what the secret meetings were about? How did He know?

Another Pharisee behind me spoke, "We aren't born of fornication. We have one Father: God."

The rulers were grabbing at anything to turn the crowds away from Jesus. They referred to Jesus as "Mary's son," instead of the customary title "Joseph's son." It was a slur on his heritage. It was rumored that Joseph hadn't married Mary until after she was with child. And the child of impurity was said to be Jesus.

I knew there had to be an explanation. And now, prophecies I hadn't considered, came to mind. Micah had prophesied, "A virgin will conceive." I almost gasped out loud. Was Jesus's father really Joseph, or was He born from a virgin and God was His Father? I listened with more interest. I would read that prophecy again with Jesus in mind.

Jesus laughed. "If God was your Father, you would love Me for I have come from God. He sent Me. You are of your father, the devil, and do the desires of your father. He murdered from the beginning, deceiving his sons with lies. I speak the truth. Can you find anything false in what I say? You don't believe My words because you are not from God."

Simon hissed, "You have a demon."

Jesus stared at Simon. His voice remained calm, but his tone was stern. "I honor My Father. You dishonor Me. If anyone keeps My word, he will never see death."

The Pharisee behind me spoke again, "Now we know You have a demon. Abraham died. The prophets died. Yet You say, 'If anyone keeps My word, he won't die?' Are you greater than our father Abraham and the prophets who died? Who are You?"

Jesus stepped toward the Pharisee behind me, isolating him from the group of rulers. "You don't know My Father. If I would tell you I don't know Him, I'd be a liar, just like you. But I do know Him, and I keep His word.

He paused; then added, "Abraham rejoiced to see My day."

Simon stepped up nose to nose with Jesus. "You're not yet fifty years old, and You've seen Abraham?"

Jesus did not flinch. "Before Abraham was born, I AM."

A hush fell over the crowd.

I hadd barely been able to breathe through the entire interchange. But now I felt like I had been punched in the gut. He was claiming to be God. "I AM" was a title given only to the God Who had saved our people from Egypt. It was the name told to Pharaoh when he had defiantly asked who had sent Moses. It was a name God had reserved for times of special displays of His greatness and power.

I blinked several times as I processed His words. Is that who Messiah would be?

I had expected the Messiah to come a certain way. This wasn't the way. I repeated the words of Micah. "A virgin will conceive." How could she conceive without God being the Father? So that would make Him God . . . . So Jesus would be the great I AM.

The other Pharisees didn't waste time in processing His words. They started picking up stones to kill Him. "What blasphemy! No one speaks of being God."

But by the time they stepped forward with their stones in hand, He had vanished!

I hadn't seen Jesus for some time. He seemed to be avoiding Jerusalem. Which was a good thing. I could feel the evil increase at the Temple. No one told me anything, but I knew they were planning evil.

A week before Passover, Jesus rode into Jerusalem on a colt.

The people praised Him, dropping palm leaves along His pathway.

My heart soared to see Him receiving the glory and praise due Him.

I had heard how the sea's waves had stilled before His voice. Was there anything He didn't control? My beliefs had been strengthened as I had searched the words of the prophets. His words and works fulfilled the prophecies. He *was* the Messiah.

Perhaps His Light would finally penetrate the darkness of the Temple.

He rode to the Temple and climbed the stairs, leaving the donkey for one of his disciples.

A group of Sadducees and Pharisees had stopped performing their duties to watch Him. "Why do you allow the people to praise you?" they demanded.

Jesus faced the people. "If the people didn't praise Me, the rocks would cry out."

I smiled. Yes, He could make them do just that. But I was glad some of His people acknowledged Him.

Later that week, the rulers found another reason to hate Jesus. Jesus had entered the Temple, their own domain, and whipped the merchants out of the Temple, saying, "My Father's House won't be made into a den of thieves."

I hadn't thought what the merchants did was wrong. We made money from their presence. The money would maintain and repair the Temple and give us a livelihood. Moses had said the people should pay a tithe to the Levites.

But now I saw that the merchants were extorting money from the people far above the required tithe. They were cheating the people. How could the money then be good? There was a lot about life I hadn't considered. Much of what we did were traditions we had made equal to the Law. I needed to sift through everything I had thought was right to see only the Law.

The rulers muttered dark threats after Jesus walked away.

They were more concerned about the money lost than the wrong of using the Temple for gain. Their darkness seemed more obvious by every ray of light Jesus showed.

Passover was coming. I prepared for the feast as masses thronged into the city. I remembered the lamb that our people had slain while in Egypt. It was at this time that they had been set free. I, too, was finding freedom. Hadn't Jesus said, "The truth shall make you free"?

After my family had completed preparations for the coming feast, we stayed inside our house, awaiting the dawn, as our ancestors had done before us.

When I arose and went to the Temple the next morning, it seemed I was the only one who had followed the rules for the feast day. No other priests were there to offer morning sacrifices. Nor, it seemed, had they stayed in their houses following the feast's preparations.

I followed the noise of the crowd.

They were at Pilate's palace, shouting, "Crucify Him!"

There had been no trial requiring crucifixion. Who did they hope to crucify?

I looked at Pilate's balcony and gasped. Could that man be Jesus? I hardly recognized Him.

He had been beaten beyond recognition.

What had happened?

When was the trial? I remembered the secret meetings, the undercurrent, but . . . my heart sank. Not during the night! Our Law prohibited any discussion before the morning sacrifices.

My morning meal churned inside me as I pushed my way through the crowd.

But His verdict was pronounced before I could make my way forward.

Jesus would be crucified.

The day progressed into more torture than I ever wanted to see.

My Savior stumbled up the hill where crucifixions took place. He couldn't even carry His own cross, He had been so badly beaten.

Spikes were driven through His hands and feet.

The soldiers lifted the cross and dropped it into the hole made to keep it upright.

When the cross hit the bottom of the hole, He gasped for air as His body jarred up and down.

I relived my dream, only this time, my hand slipped from His grasp and I was falling with no one to save me. How could He save anyone if He died? Would He preform some miracle and jump down from the cross?

Even as I thought, one of the chief rulers heckled Him. "You said You could destroy the Temple and rebuild it in three days; but you can't even save Yourself!"

Others joined in. "If You are the Son of God, come down from the cross."

All the Pharisees, Sadducees, and chief priests had come to watch. As if evil had won.

They all had something to tell Him, now that He wouldn't respond and embarrass them. "He saved others. He can't save Himself."

"Let Him come down from the cross if He's the King of Israel."

"Then we'll believe."

They laughed as if they'd won.

How could they win, when they were killing the Son of God? Our own Messiah?

I stepped away from them. I wouldn't be associated with their torments. I stopped listening to their jeering. I stood under the cross and bowed my head, my sorrow too great to even shed tears.

I felt a drop and looked at my hand. His blood. The drop of blood had come from His hands as He pushed against them to raise Himself up to breathe.

One look at his pale face told me He was near death.

I looked back at the drop in my hand, as if by holding it I could keep Him alive. The tears I had not been able to spill before, slowly escaped my eyes now.

He was dying.

My Savior was dying, and I could do nothing.

What would happen to the light He had told me to be? The light that shone in the dark corners where evil lived. How could I continue to shine, when He, the ultimate Light, was dead?

He cried with a loud voice, interrupting my thoughts, "It is finished."

When men died, they spoke with a weak voice. They didn't get louder. But His voice rang out as if He had conquered death. What did it mean?

They were His last words. He lowered His head and was gone . . . as if He had given Himself over to death.

I was relieved He wouldn't suffer any more.

I stood there, alone.

I thought of Passover, so much on my mind in the past few days. Now I lacked any enthusiasm to even complete it. The meal all Israel observed, to know and remember how God had provided salvation to His people in Egypt. He had rescued them.

And in all these years since then, He hadn't forgotten them. He had sent His prophets. Even then, His prophets had been mistreated. Look at Jeremiah! Staying in prison because he foretold of our nation's captivity.

Now, God had sent the Messiah to save His people. Only this time, the sacrifice was His Only Son. Isn't that what Jesus had tried to tell me? That God loved us so much that He would sacrifice His Son?

How could His sacrifice save me?

He was perfect, just like the lamb of the Passover had to be.

The Law couldn't show God's care and love. It was stern, unyielding. It showed how much man fell short of what God wanted. The Father's Son was paying the cost of the Law's penalty. He was the perfect, sinless Lamb sacrificed for me. Isn't that what John the Baptist had called Him, "The Lamb of God, Who takes away the sin of the world"?

What had Jesus said? "God so loved the world that He gave His Only Son."

He gave His life.

Evil didn't take it from Him.

Why?

He gave it up so I could have eternal life. Not life in the physical world, but life in the spiritual. That's what He meant when He said that we wouldn't die.

Moses had that spiritual relationship with God. A relationship so complete and whole that he saw God. The craving in his heart had been filled with knowing God and being in His presence.

That's what I wanted. That relationship with God that allowed a communion of spirits: His Spirit with mine.

Even in the midst of my sorrow, and the tears that still streaked my face, I was getting closer to finding that communion with God's Spirit.

The sun turned as black as the darkest night.

Thunder crashed. Lightning exploded.

The top of the hill where the crosses stood was a known target for lightning to strike.

Others around me were fleeing.

If I had cared for myself at that point, I would have run to safety. But I wouldn't leave His side.

The soldiers were anxious to leave the hill. They broke the legs of the two criminals on either side of Jesus.

But the centurion stopped his soldier when he approached Jesus. He took the javelin from his sergeant and thrust it into Jesus's side.

The pressure of fluids in His body poured water and blood down the handle of the javelin, pooling at my feet as I stood beside the centurion.

His blood poured out, like the blood of the lamb I killed every year to cover my sin. But this blood would not need to be poured out again and again. This sacrifice was once for all. Complete. Enough. It would take away my wrong, as far as the east is from the west.

The crowds were gone.

The darkness covered their deeds. The rain fell in torrents, washing the blood from His body to flow in gullies down the hill.

I lingered, unable to leave His body.

I touched his foot, washed by the rain. It was cold. Lifeless.

I was alone.

The Law spoke of any man who hung on a tree being cursed. I felt mankind was cursed. Jesus had taken our curse on Him.

Our Law declared no man should hang overnight.

I went to Pilate, hoping he would grant me permission to take Jesus's body and bury it.

When I entered Pilate's chamber, he was pacing like a wild animal.

Did he even know I was there?

"May I have the body of Jesus to bury?"

Pilate stopped pacing and glanced at me for the first time. His eyes looked haunted. He shrugged, as if that was the least of his worries. "Yes."

I waited for further instructions.

He gave none.

Joseph of Arimathea met me at the cross. Everyone else had gone. "I have my tomb."

I nodded.

Between the two of us, we lifted the cross out of the hole and laid it on the ground. We unbound His body from the wood. Jesus's body was light; all his blood had been poured out. I thought again of the lamb's sacrifice. No blood was left.

We didn't speak as we wrapped it in linen grave clothes and carried it to the hillside where Joseph had prepared for his own burial.

I was grateful for Joseph's help. It seemed to lessen my grief as we shared the task.

I can't remember all we did. I numbly went through the preparations for His body. I was exhausted when we finished, but He had been buried.

After stumbling my way home, I fell into bed, but couldn't sleep.

My Savior was dead.

Where would Israel look for hope now?

When the morning came, it required great effort to go to the Temple. I didn't want to face the rulers. I wanted to scream and curse them. How could they?

But when I saw them, I remembered Jesus's words. "Men love darkness rather than Light, because their deeds are evil." They were so absorbed in their darkness they couldn't even recognize the Light. Evil held their hearts so tightly they didn't see God.

I pitied them.

Somehow I wandered through the next few days. When I heard a group of His followers were meeting. I went to the room where they were gathered together. They were fishermen, disciples, even a harlot Jesus had forgiven in the Temple when the rulers had demanded her judgment.

When I entered, some gave me hateful looks; others whispered to those beside them.

They locked the door behind me. Were they afraid the rulers would come after them? They had nothing to fear from me. I wouldn't report them. I wanted to know more of God.

It was almost like we couldn't believe Jesus was dead. What were we to do now?

Even with standing room only, no one spoke.

When I heard a collective gasp, I looked toward the front of the room. Jesus stood there. Had He entered through the locked door? I glanced back at the bolted door; then again at Jesus. He smiled.

The tension in my shoulders relaxed. I took a breath I didn't know I was holding.

He was alive.

I didn't just listen to His words; I absorbed them. I wanted to know God. I followed His every movement, hanging on every word.

He explained how the Scriptures pointed to Him. He told how His work provided clearance to God.

I smiled. I understood now how the Law's sacrifices represented what He did. He wanted the sweet sacrifice of my life given back to Him.

When I returned to the Temple for evening sacrifices, Simon met me at the door. I sighed. I didn't want to fight with him today. I wanted to worship God. But he stood in my way, keeping me from entering. "Nicodemus." His voice was urgent, which got my attention.

I struggled to keep the irritation out of my tone. "What is it?"

Simon lowered his voice, "The curtain of the Holiest of Holy."

I didn't have time for this game. Why didn't he just tell me? "What about it?"

"It was ripped from top to bottom."

"Top to bottom?" The curtain was layers thick. I looked at him.

Simon nodded, as if he needed me to believe him. "It was during the crucifixion—when the lightning struck."

I nodded. We walked toward the room where the curtain hung. It kept everyone away from God, protecting them, so God's judgment wouldn't fall on them. I stood before the curtain, wanting to touch it, but feeling the holiness of the room beyond it.

The high priest entered the Holiest of Holy only once a year, with a sacrifice for the people. His foot was tied with a rope in case the sacrifice wasn't acceptable and God smote him dead. The other priests would be able to pull out his body without entering themselves.

The room represented the presence of God. He lived there.

The lightning had struck, burning such a tear that the curtain could never be brought back together again.

The opening invited anyone to enter.

As I looked into the room, a breeze blew across my cheek. How could the wind blow here?

I saw the Ark of the Covenant, made from the purest of gold. Two golden cherubs held their wings outstretched over the mercy seat. The cloud of God had rested on the Ark when our people had moved from Egypt to our Promised Land. I had always felt this replica, made after we had returned from captivity, lacked God's Spirit. Like He was holding back, waiting for something.

I felt that breeze again. Was His Spirit moving His people to know Him?

I had felt this same stirring while listening to Jesus in that crowded room. His Words invited us to come, to know Him.

It would never be the same—offering sacrifices, burning incense, bringing our offerings to the Temple.

He was the sacrifice. And He was enough.

I felt His presence, not because I could see into the Holiest of Holy, but because I could come before Him.

I fell to my knees on that hard marble floor, like I should have done at the cross. I had been too numb to do it then. But now, I worshiped my Savior and my God Who had made the way through His death for me to come into His presence ad truly know Him.

I am Andrew, Brother of Peter

⚜

EVERYONE REMEMBERS PETER. He was always talking, always doing something to stand out in the crowd. He was one of the inner circle of Jesus's disciples. But me? People never noticed me. I was the quiet one. Peter's little brother. The tag-along. The one without any thoughts of his own. Or that's what people assumed.

PETER HAD A way with words. He's the one who proclaimed, "You're the Christ, the Son of God." Jesus commended him for that. I wished I'd said it. We all knew it was true. But Peter said it. I was in the background, like always.

Of course, Peter's words could get him into trouble too. But I knew how to come alongside him and get him out of it—most of the time. After Peter had made the merchants angry, trying to make them pay more for our haul of fish, I told him, "Let me talk to them. We need the sales." Peter didn't argue. He knew I was right.

John the Baptizer foretold about Jesus's coming. In fact, I followed John first, until he pointed out Jesus as the Lamb of God. After he baptized Jesus, I left John. Normally I'm loyal to an extreme. Hadn't I always stuck with Peter when his mouth got us both in trouble when we were little? But when John the Baptizer pointed out Jesus, it was as if he was urging me to leave him and follow Christ instead.

I didn't want to. I was torn. John had preached repentance. I could do that. But Jesus preached peace. Who could live at peace with Peter? But I I respected John, and he was telling me to follow Jesus. So I did. And it wasn't long before I was urging Peter, "Come with me. We've found the Messiah!"

When we came to Jesus for the first time, Jesus noticed Peter, "You are Simon the son of John, but now your name will be Peter." Jesus said nothing to me.

When we were leaving the Temple, I noticed the architecture and thought it would be something I could talk about, hoping Jesus would recognize my appreciation for God's house. "What wonderful stones and buildings!"

Jesus looked beyond the Temple and said, "Not one stone will be left upon another. All will be torn down."

That wasn't what I was expecting, but it did get my attention. What more could the Romans do to us Jews? What should we do to be ready? I stayed close to Jesus to hear if He would say more.

He didn't.

While sitting at the Mount of Olives with Peter, James, and John, I couldn't wait any longer. I had to know. "What's going to happen with the Temple? When will we see the destruction You mentioned?"

Jesus said, "Many will spread rumors, cause wars. There'll be earthquakes and famines."

I clenched my hands into fists.

Jesus touched my shoulder, reassuring me. "Be on guard. You will suffer."

I tried to look confident, but I didn't' feel it. "What should we do?"

Jesus looked right at me. "Don't fear what you will say. When the time comes, you will know."

His answer was personal. I knew He had seen my biggest fear, and He had answered it.

I searched Jesus's face for more direction. His eyes reflected a peace only He could give. They told me more than His next words, "God will give you the words."

I lowered my eyes. I wasn't a speaker. I would have to trust His peace would come. I didn't feel it now, even without suffering.

"God will give me the words."

I pondered Jesus's words. At first I was despondent over them. I never was good in school and hadn't attended much in our small Galilee village. People held my interest more than books. I didn't talk like Peter, but I could listen. And now I listened to Jesus as He gave us answers, even before I could ask the questions. He was preparing all of us for what was to come.

Those words came back to me many days after that talk.

Peter was always jumping out of the boat—even to the point of walking on water. How would it feel to do that? Like you were floating on air? Or did you roll like thunder across the sky, only in the waves of the sea? When I asked Peter, Peter couldn't even remember, he had been so busy talking!

The people gathered to listen to Jesus. This was the biggest crowd ever!

I didn't like crowds. I preferred the quiet times when Jesus talked just to us. But I understood the people's thirst for Christ's words.

I stretched to see all the people who had come to find healing in His words.

A lad pushed his way through the crowd, trying to get closer to Jesus. No one would let him.

I remembered Jesus's rebuke to us about letting the children come to him. I left my place beside Jesus and moved through the crowd to reach the boy.

"What have you got?"

The lad held out his lunch. "Mom sent me to listen, so I could tell her the words of the Teacher. She couldn't come."

I smiled. "Follow me." I led the boy to stand beside Jesus.

As we reached Jesus's side, I overheard Jesus asking Philip, "Where are we to buy bread, so that these may eat?"

Philip looked over the crowd. "Two hundred denarii worth of bread is not enough for so many people."

I nudged the lad ahead of me. "Here's a lad who has brought five barley loaves and two fish, but what are these for so many people?"

Jesus nodded at me and laid his hand on the lad's shoulder. He turned to us. "Tell the people to sit." He showed us what he could do with so little. And the entire crowd was fed.

Nothing more is said of me in the Gospels until the disciples huddled in the upper room after Jesus died.

I didn't get attention. I just listened to Jesus and brought others to Him.

The promise of Jesus settled in my heart. "God will give you the words."

Before Jesus left, he told us, "All authority has been given to Me in heaven and on earth. Go and make disciples of all the nations, baptizing them, and teaching them to observe all that I commanded you."

Peter became the spokesman in Jerusalem. I was just Peter's brother.

I didn't stay in Jerusalem with the other disciples. I went out into the world to bring people to Jesus. But the words of Jesus stayed with me. "I am with you always, even to the end of the age."

Tradition says Andrew debated with the Roman proconsul in Greece. He was given many chances to deny his faith, to forsake his God, to change his words. Instead he spoke about God Who became a man in order to save all people.

Since he would not change his words that God gave him, the proconsul condemned him to death.

The Romans were known for their cruelty. They ruled the world.

So Andrew was crucified, not on a normal cross, but on a cross in the shape of an "X" to make breathing more difficult.

Instead of pounding nails into his hands, they tied them. Maybe he requested this so he wouldn't have hands like his Savior's. But by having his hands tied, he suffered longer. He hung on the cross two days before he died. With each breath, he struggled to lift his body up against the pull of gravity, grab a breath, and fall against his feet and hands.

Tradition tells us during those final two days he hung on the cross, he preached to those who would hear.

Do you know what he preached?

God gave him the words.

Do you have the right words to say? Do your words point people to Jesus?

God will give you the words. Listen to Him.

I am John,
the Beloved Disciple

I am John, son of Zebedee, from Capernaum of Galilee.

I was fishing, with my brother James, when we first heard John the Baptizer preaching. We had sailed our fishing boat toward the Jordan River, where its mouth pours into the Sea of Galilee.

John's voice carried over the water. "Repent, for the Kingdom of God is here."

He wasn't afraid to tell anyone—religious leaders, soldiers, tax collectors, whoever would listen—that they needed to repent. He had the courage I'd always wanted, so I told James I wanted to find out more about this man.

James and I rowed our boat closer so we could hear.

We argued over where to dock the boat. James always told me what to do, as if I hadn't been fishing four years already.

I followed John the Baptizer that day. And I repented.

But even by repenting, I found my heart hadn't changed. James was still as annoying as he'd always been. And he followed John the Baptizer with me. So my annoyance followed me.

John the Baptizer told everyone what they did wrong.

I could relate to that. My brother told me what I did wrong every day. If he didn't, my father did. He demanded perfection and expected it too! When my father corrected me with his calloused, sea-worn hands, I wouldn't say it was gentle or loving, but I did it right the next time.

One day, we saw John baptize a Man he called the Lamb of God. Afterwards, he told us to follow the Man.

Following Jesus was like following a friend, who knew what I needed. I clung to Him. James told me I was annoying, that I stuck to Jesus like one of those barnacles we scraped off the bottom of our boats. But Jesus didn't mind; maybe He knew I needed it. He loved me. I could feel it in His touch.

Many others also wanted to feel the healing touch of His hands. Every day, people thronged to Him to be healed.

One day, an important official of the synagogue approached, begging Jesus to heal his daughter.

Before Jesus acknowledged the man, He looked at the crowd around him, asking, "Who touched Me?"

No one said anything. Many looked down as if they were guilty.

Finally, Peter said, "Master, the people crowd around you. Anyone could have brushed against You."

But Jesus studied a woman whose head was bowed. "Someone touched Me, and power has left Me."

The woman fell trembling at His feet. "Master, I had a bleeding disease twelve years. I've spent all I had for help. No one could help me. I thought if I could touch the hem of Your tunic, I'd be healed."

I could relate. Sometimes I felt if I could just slip into Jesus's skin, I could be whole. I held my breath. What would Jesus tell her?

James bumped into me. I looked at him, irritably. His eyes said, "Get away and find your own skin." I shook my head and moved closer to Jesus.

Jesus raised the woman to her feet. "Daughter, your faith has made you well. Be at peace."

I breathed again. I felt cleaner, as if I had been the one with the disease, waiting for rebuke, but instead receiving commendation. How could the Master always show love?

During this entire time, the official had waited.

Now a servant approached him. "Jairus, there's no need for the Master."

Jairus brows creased as he studied his servant's face. "Is she . . ." He couldn't say it.

The servant finished for him, nodding. "Dead."

Jairus's shoulders slumped. In spite of the crowds, he covered his face and wept.

Jesus touched Jairus's arm. "Don't be afraid. Believe. She'll be made well."

Jairus walked with Jesus to his house. When we reached his courtyard, he hesitated, taking a deep breath before entering.

Jesus turned to those gathered, "Stop weeping. She hasn't died. She's only sleeping."

The people jeered, mocking Him.

I clenched my hands and bit my lip. How dare they laugh at Jesus!

Jesus led us—Peter, James and me—into the room with the girl's father and shut the door behind us.

My eyes adjusted to the darkened room. Only a sliver of light entered through a small, round, high window. A woman held a girl in her lap. She was weeping.

The girl's body was limp, like a fish removed from the water. Her face and neck had already started stiffening in death.

Jairus knelt beside them. He took the girl's hand in his own. His tears mixed with the woman's as they wept over the girl.

I shivered. I didn't like touching anything dead, even fish. I didn't hover near Jesus this time, but crossed my arms and leaned against the wall by the door. I wanted distance from death and its sorrow. I would have slipped out the door but remembered the people who had mocked. I'd wait and watch.

Jesus took the girl's other hand. "Child, arise."

The little girl stood up.

If I hadn't been in the room, I wouldn't have believed it. I blinked. Had I actually seen her dead?

Jairus and his wife looked at each other and laughed. They hugged the girl.

Jairus turned toward Jesus.

I will never forget his look. It was one of trust, love, and worship, all in one glance.

Jairus reached toward Jesus, as if he didn't know whether to hug Jesus or fall at his feet in worship. The girl decided for him. "I'm hungry."

Jesus motioned to the girl. "She needs something to eat."

Jairus laughed again, hugging the girl.

We followed the girl from the room. She helped her mother prepare a meal for all of us.

Those who had mocked Jesus now laughed with joy. And I hoped also with embarrassment for their unbelief.

As we were entering another city, I noticed someone casting out demons. He wasn't one of us.

I approached him. What made him think he had the right to do Jesus's work? "Stop!" I demanded.

He looked over my shoulder at Jesus. His expression was one of confusion.

Jesus placed his hand on my shoulder, but met the man's gaze. "Don't hinder him; for if he's not against you, he's for you."

I dropped my head, embarrassed. I had only tried to protect Jesus. As if He needed defended. I had trouble accepting anyone who wasn't with us. How could he obey God, but not follow Him? Shouldn't everyone who loved Jesus follow Him like I did?

Jesus was always showing me a different way.

Another time, we were walking through Samaria to Jerusalem. Most Jews crossed the Jordan River twice rather than pass through Samaria. Samaritans weren't pure-blooded Jews, so true Jews wouldn't associate with them. I wanted to remind Jesus of this, but after his rebuke about those casting out demons, I thought I'd better not.

Normally someone from the crowd would offer us lodging and meals. But here, no one received Him. What was wrong with these people! Didn't they know Who Jesus was? They should have been begging Him to eat at their house. The day was almost over and still no one had offered. I told Jesus, "They have no respect for You. You should command fire to come down from heaven and consume them!"

Jesus looked at me.

In that look, I felt rebuked. I lowered my head.

He explained, "You don't know what kind of spirit you have. The Son of Man didn't come to destroy lives, but to save them."

What kind of spirit did I have? Weren't these people disobedient to the Law of Moses? Hadn't they intermarried with the heathen and become impure? Hadn't they rejected Jesus by not even giving Him a meal?

But that idea of saving them kept coming back as I watched Jesus show love by his touch, his words, and his actions.

The next time we passed through Samaria, I didn't question Jesus, but agreed to purchase provisions when nobody offered us food. We left Jesus to rest at the well while we went to the market place. When we returned, He was talking to a woman who was obviously a sinner. Why was He talking to this kind of woman? Didn't He know she was tainted?

But she brought the entire city to see Jesus.

I was quick to judge.

Jesus was quicker to show love.

Later, I asked, "What did you tell that woman?"

He smiled. "I made her thirsty enough to come."

I didn't understand.

I didn't understand, either, when Jesus led Peter, James, and me to the top of a mountain, leaving the other disciples at the bottom to heal and cast out demons. We had reached the summit. As I caught my breath from the climb, I looked at Jesus, expecting some lesson. But He didn't speak. Instead, His face began to shine like the sun and His garments radiated white light.

I couldn't continue to look at Him. The brightness almost blinded me. What was happening? I wanted to stand closer to Him, but was afraid the white light would burn me. Would He leave us, like Enoch or Elijah?

As I watched, Moses and Elijah appeared. They talked with Jesus.

I strained to hear what they said, but felt forced to stay back from the light. Its intensity glowed around them, as if God had stepped down from heaven.

Peter, never lacking words, interrupted them, "Should we make three tabernacles to worship?"

Before he received an answer, a cloud hovered over us. Through the mist, I heard God's voice, "This is My beloved Son, with whom I am well pleased. Listen to Him!"

I fell trembling to my face. Would we live? Only Moses had seen God face to face, and only Elijah and Enoch had escaped death to live with Him. We were in the presence of God's glorified Son! And we had heard the voice of God. How could we live?

I lay with my face to the ground, unable to look again at the glory.

Time seemed to stop until someone touched my shoulder. I timidly raised my head.

It was Jesus.

Moses and Elijah were gone. And so were the cloud and the bright light.

We were alone. Just Jesus, Peter, James and I.

I couldn't speak. I stood on trembling legs. What did it mean?

Jesus was ready to leave the mountain.

I followed, glad that I could see something normal again. What would I tell the other disciples? Wouldn't they be jealous?

Jesus paused in our descent. He looked at me, as if he could read my thoughts. "Tell no one what you've seen, until the Son of Man has risen from the dead."

I swallowed but nodded. It'd be hard not to share what glory we had seen. I touched my face. Did it shine, like Moses's when he had been with God on the mountain of Sinai? What if they asked? I shook my head. I had told the Lord I wouldn't tell.

Peter must have felt like me, bursting to tell the others. He tried to make sense of what we'd seen, asking Jesus, "Why did the prophets say Elijah must come first?"

Jesus nodded. "Elijah must restore all things. But he's already come. They killed him."

I thought of John the Baptist. He had foretold of Jesus. His own people had missed the signs. He had been hated by the Pharisees and beheaded by Herod. I had mourned his loss, but the people he had come to warn hadn't. What would they do to Jesus, if they killed His prophet who foretold of Him? I didn't want to know.

As if Jesus read my mind, Jesus continued. "The Son of Man will suffer."

Somehow I knew that the great vision on the mountain was a gift of light before great darkness, The sense of pride fled, leaving a pit in my gut. Suffering would soon come to all of us. I wasn't ready.

James and I lay rolled up in our cloaks on the cooling sand by the beach. The crowds had gone home. The sun had set. Our feet were stretched toward the fire we had cooked our fish. The other disciples had already fallen asleep. The day had been long. James whispered, "What did the Lord mean when he said the Son of Man must rise from the dead?"

To rise from the dead meant He'd die. I didn't want to think about that. I had just met Jesus. He was showing me God. Not just God, but what God expected me to be. If Jesus died, how would I know what to do? Maybe Jesus was sharing with us, so we could prevent it, stop His suffering. I didn't answer James. I had no answer. But I intended to stay close to Jesus to prevent any harm coming to Him. I rolled away from James, hoping to fall asleep. Instead my mind kept churning.

But the answers didn't come.

It was the first day of Unleavened Bread. Jesus didn't tell us where we'd celebrate it. Shouldn't we be preparing for it? When the other disciples were busy, he told Peter and me to go ahead of them. "When you enter the city, follow a man with a pitcher. Ask the owner of the house, 'Where is the guest room in which I may eat the Passover with My disciples?' He'll show you. Prepare for us there."

Peter and I hurried ahead to make preparations.

When the others arrived, Jesus seemed withdrawn, quiet.

I felt rebuffed by His quietness. What had happened while I was gone? When I asked James, he just shrugged.

We were ready to partake of the Passover. We sat around the circle on cushions. I squeezed in beside Jesus.

Before He began the meal, Jesus took a basin, and washed our feet. Was this why He was upset? Because I hadn't found a servant to do this? I hadn't had time. We'd been busy getting the meal ready.

But here he was, doing a servant's task.

I didn't know what to say. I just let Him wash my feet.

Peter always had something to say. He didn't want Jesus to touch his feet.

But Jesus said, "If I don't wash you, then you'll have no part with Me."

I was glad I'd kept my mouth shut.

Peter kept talking, "Don't just wash my feet, but wash all of me."

I could understand his feeling. I wanted to be totally a part of whatever Jesus did, too.

"Only your feet need to be cleaned." Jesus laid down at the table after putting aside the wash basin and towel. He spoke of serving one another.

I looked at James. Serving? If James ever served me, I'd be surprised.

Jesus said, "One of you will betray Me."

I should have been thinking about how I'd protect Him from suffering, but I only wanted to know who would betray him. I leaned against Him. "Who?"

He nodded toward the circle. "I'll give the bread to the one."

I watched, ready to judge. Because of the way Jesus had been so private about telling me, I didn't want to confront the man now. But I would later.

Jesus broke the bread and blessed it.

When He passed it to Judas, I had to remind myself to shut my mouth. Judas? He was our treasurer. We trusted him with our money. He'd even tithed our money. Or had he? I questioned everything now.

Could Jesus be mistaken? How would Judas betray Him?

Jesus gestured for Judas to leave. "What you must do, do quickly."

Judas studied Jesus for a moment before he left.

Did he leave to pay for what we had prepared? I hadn't taken money to cover the Passover preparations, but the owner of the room had offered without money. Judas probably went to pay what we owed.

His future betrayal troubled me, but I'd talk with him later and convince him of his wrong. I cringed. Judas wasn't one of the disciples I felt comfortable approaching. He kept himself distant. I'd thought it was because of his education and his Zealot tendencies. But it had always seemed as if Jesus trusted him, so I had too.

I shook my head and turned my attention to the discussion of the others were having. James was talking about serving in God's Kingdom.

I interrupted him, "You should serve me in His Kingdom."

James, not to be outdone by me, said, "Over my dead body."

I asked Andrew, "Who do you think should be the greatest in Christ's Kingdom?"

Jesus put His arm on my shoulder.

When my father did that, he was about to reprimand me. I expected it now. I flinched, feeling my face flush. What had I done now?

Jesus shook his head. "The kings of the earth vie for power over each another. But not so with you. The one who wants to be great, let him be like the youngest."

I looked over at James and nodded. I was the youngest of the disciples.

James shrugged like he didn't care. But I knew he did. He always had to be better than I.

But Jesus didn't stop there. "Lead like a servant. For who is greater, the one who reclines at the table, or the one who serves?"

I raised my eyebrow at James. Who was leaning on the Master's bosom? Me. I would be the leader.

Still Jesus wasn't finished. "I am among you as the One who serves."

James mimicked me with his raised eyebrows and laughed.

"My Father granted Me a kingdom. I grant you the right to join Me at My table. You will sit on thrones judging the tribes of Israel."

I leaned back. Yes! I'd be a leader.

We finished the meal and sang the closing song of the Passover. Our voices blended together, acknowledging God as our Provider and our Redeemer from the bondage of Egypt.

I never considered the contradiction of fighting over who would be the greatest, then telling God He was the greatest. I was slow to learn.

It was late when we finished. The sun had already set, and darkness had taken over. We followed Jesus to the Garden of Gethsemane. I liked going to the Garden. It was where Jesus would explain things to us, away from the crowds.

But tonight seemed different.

Jesus was quiet. He told us, "Pray that you won't fall into temptation."

Temptation? What temptation would we face that we couldn't overcome?

He encouraged Peter, James, and me to follow Him further. We could still see the others. Jesus seemed depressed. I had never seen Him anxious about anything. But tonight He was. He told us, "Watch with Me."

I began in earnest to pray for Him. What kind of prayer could the Son of God need? Why was Jesus so distressed? What temptation would we face that we couldn't conquer?

As I prayed, the lateness of the night and the heaviness of the food settled over me and made me sleepy. I rubbed my eyes and tried to focus. Jesus was taking a long time. How long would he pray? I thought about Judas. How should I confront him? My thoughts drifted.

I woke with a start. Jesus had returned. He nudged me with his foot. I must have fallen asleep in spite of the Lord needing my prayers. I yawned.

"Couldn't you watch with Me for one hour? Pray you don't give in to temptation. The spirit is willing, but the flesh is weak."

He went farther into the darkness of the garden. I could see His form kneeling.

I tried to stay awake. I thought of prayer. When I listened to the scribes and teachers pray in the synagogue on the Sabbath, I often grew tired, even when it was morning. Jesus had explained that prayer was talking with His Father.

I cringed. When I talked with my father, I prayed he'd be in a good mood. I shook my head. This wasn't praying. Jesus didn't need us too many times. But He seemed to need us tonight.

I began the prayer like Jesus had taught us. "Our Father in heaven." What kind of temptation would Jesus not be able to help us through? Again my eyes grew heavy. That was good lamb. It was good to be around Jesus. People gave him the best they had. Not the scrawny lambs my family always had to purchase for Passover. It was hard to focus when I had eaten so much.

I felt Jesus come back a second time and nudge me awake. But I must have just gone back to sleep. He made sure I was awake when He came the third time. "Get up." He urged us. "The one who betrays Me is at hand."

I woke with a start. The one who betrays Him? Was it to be tonight then? I hadn't even confronted Judas yet.

I saw a glow of torches enter the Garden and approach us. I heard the brushing of armor as soldiers marched. How many were coming?

My drowsiness was gone. I was wide awake.

I watched the flickering light as it came toward us. When I could focus on faces, I could see Judas leading them.

I swallowed. I didn't know what to feel. Disbelief? Anger? How could Judas do this? He'd been one of us. He'd eaten with us as we had learned about God. Why would he turn on Jesus? This betrayal was more than just over money. Had he betrayed Jesus to Rome? For what?

Those next moments seem etched in my mind. Time dragged out like years.

I couldn't believe all the Roman soldiers. They needed that many soldiers? Their torches lit up the night as if it were day. Only the shadows lingered, hiding those who didn't want to be seen.

I remained by Jesus, though unsure what I could do against this much force.

In spite of his shameful deed, Judas greeted Jesus with a kiss, as if everything was normal. How could he do this to Him? Things I hadn't noticed before now stuck out. How Judas had sharpened his dagger, even as Jesus explained about loving our neighbor. Had he even listened to the Master? But even as I thought of Judas, I remembered my command to call down fire on an entire city.

I looked at the other disciples. Some had stepped back from the light of the torches, their faces hidden in shadows. What could we do? There was no stopping Rome, when they brought their soldiers. But when they came, they always brought destruction. How could I protect Jesus from them?

I watched, unable to breathe, as Judas kissed the Lord.

I wanted to smack Judas. He kissed Him, like he was greeting a friend. But even more, frustrating was Jesus's response. He expected it. He knew it. The look in His eyes was not condemnation, but of resignation, and a strength I couldn't fathom.

I looked at the other disciples. What could we do? How could we stop this? But some of the disciples had already fled. Others stood hidden in the shadows, beyond the torches' reach.

Jesus asked, "Who are you looking for?"

The centurion beside Judas answered, "Jesus of Nazareth."

What had He done? We showed no rebellion toward Rome. What charge could they bring? There must be some mistake.

Jesus said, "I Am He."

And suddenly, the Roman soldiers fell to the ground. Just as I had fallen before God's voice at the top of the mountain. Who could stand before His presence and not fall down?

To hear hundreds of soldiers, with their armor clanking and clamoring to the ground, was like hearing a battle. Jesus would not be taken. He had just proven Who He was.

I stood taller. Rome would not get the best of Jesus. Nor would Judas. I would see to Judas later.

But my elation didn't last long. Even as the soldiers returned to their feet, they stepped forward to seize Him.

I shouldn't say that . . . They could never take Jesus.

He gave Himself. Isn't that what Jesus had told us earlier—He was a servant? I didn't understand, nor did I want to.

Anger rose from my toes. I could feel my skin tingle. I clenched my fists, felt my face flush, knew I would explode if Judas even looked at me.

He didn't. He kept his head down, as if he hadn't caused all of this.

My anger burned not just toward Judas, but toward these soldiers and whoever had sent them . . . Was that the servant of Joseph Caiaphas, the high priest? Was he involved in this? Our family made sure his family always had the best fish!

Peter, always impetuous, swung his sword. Where he even got it, I don't know. He certainly didn't know how to use it. All he managed to do was cut off the ear of someone standing by Judas. Too bad he didn't strike Judas instead.

In contrast to my anger, Jesus showed loved. He bent down, found the piece of ear in the dirt, and attached it to the man's head again, without even a word.

I could only shake my head. Jesus always served. Showing me what love was.

They bound Jesus's hands behind his back and took him away.

I watched until their light could not be seen. I looked around the darkness for the other disciples. I was alone.

Why hadn't I stood with Jesus? Shame crept up my face.

Keeping in the shadows, I followed them to the palace of Joseph Caiaphas. His courtyard was lit with torches, as if he was expecting this meeting.

I entered, staying in the shadows. I must know what they did to my Lord.

As the night progressed, I gained enough courage to step toward one of the fires. I warmed my hands, but the coldness of the night seemed to penetrate more than my hands. My very heart was chilled by the evil that was happening around me.

None of the religious leaders liked Jesus. They had always asked questions to trip him up. His answers always showed their wrong.

They hated Him. But were afraid of what the people thought. Now, without the crowds present, what would they do?

I yawned and stretched. I was tired, but I couldn't sleep if I wanted to. How could I stay awake now, when I hadn't been able to stay awake to pray?

I noticed Peter standing by another fire pit. I nodded to him, as if in silent acknowledgement that we stood together for our Lord. I searched the shadows for any of the other disciples. I saw none.

A servant approached Peter. "You were with Jesus, the Galilean."

Peter shook his head, muttering, "I don't know what you're talking about." He turned quickly and caught my expression, then looked down.

The girl nodded, but I could tell she didn't believe him.

Would I also be asked? What would I say? My insides turned like a fish caught in the net.

I moved away from Peter and leaned against a tree in the shadows. Now I could hear, but not be seen. I didn't want to be around anyone I knew. The courtyard was big, and a lot of people came and went.

Another servant spoke to a gathering around some benches. He pointed to Peter. "He's one of them."

Peter swore. "No, I'm not! I don't know the Man." He turned away.

There were reasons why it was better to be quiet in a crowd. Peter stood out. He was always talking, spilling his thoughts. With Jesus, he would ask question everyone else thought, but no one had the courage to ask. People remembered him.

They must not have remembered me. I was glad. What would I say?

Another servant girl pointed at Peter. "You were with that Man in the Garden. You cut off my uncle's ear."

Peter cursed. "I don't know the Man!"

Immediately a rooster crowed.

Peter's face flushed red. Realization of what he had just done showed in his face. He staggered from the room. As he passed me, I saw his tears. He could barely keep his composure till he reached the gate of the courtyard.

I remembered the Lord's words, "Before a rooster crows, you will deny Me three times." What could I tell him?

What had the Lord said about me? I tried to remember. I had been so busy fighting with James over who would be the greatest in His Kingdom and who would be my servant, that I didn't remember what He had said. If Peter could deny Jesus, what would I do?

I thought of Judas betraying Jesus, of Peter denying Him. And here I was, standing, hovering in the shadows, hoping no one would even speak to me. If these were who Jesus depended upon, what hope did He have?

I paced. My meager prayers seemed too late.

The night wore on. A door opened.

Soldiers emerged, dragging Jesus, His hands tied behind Him like a criminal's.

What could a world do, when they held their God in their hands?

Evil intent was etched in the faces of the elders as they followed the soldiers.

I followed from a distance.

Their torches led the way to Pilate's courtroom. The soldiers took Jesus into Pilate's palace, while the Jews clustered under the balcony where Pilate would present his verdict.

What cause would they have to bring Jesus to Pilate? He had done nothing against Rome.

I leaned against the wall in the back corner of the courtyard and folded my arms, straining to hear what they plotted. Anger etched dark lines on their faces recounting embarrassment when Jesus had disgraced them in public. Voices rose, rehearsing failed attempts to crush Jesus.

When Pilate stepped out onto his balcony, he raised his arms for attention. A hush fell over the waiting group. "What accusation do you bring against this Man?" Pilate demanded.

It took them a moment to refocus. One Pharisee raised his voice, "If this Man weren't an evildoer, we wouldn't have brought Him to you."

What kind of brazen response was that? If I had answered my father like that, I'd have been slapped across the face!

Pilate looked at the sky for a moment. The partial moon had risen as the night waned. He leaned over the balcony. I could tell, he was irritated at having been roused in the night and didn't want anything to do with this case. "Judge Him according to your Law."

"We aren't permitted to put anyone to death."

I gasped. Was that what they wanted?

Pilate pulled his toga more tightly around him, for the chill of the night, or maybe as a nervous gesture, I wasn't sure. "What has He done?"

I opened my lips to call out, "He's done nothing." But the words stuck. I couldn't spit them out. I licked my lips and looked around.

"We found this man misleading our nation, forbidding to pay taxes to Caesar, and saying He is Christ, a King."

Pilate turned to Jesus. "Are You the King of the Jews?"

Jesus answered, "It is as you say."

Pilate seemed to evaluate Jesus's words for a long moment. A firm resolution settled over his face as he again faced the men. "I find no fault with Him."

But the leaders insisted. "He stirs up the people, teaching even in Galilee."

Pilate asked, "He's from Galilee?"

They nodded.

Pilate motioned to the guards. "Take Him to Herod."

They led Jesus away.

I swallowed the bile that lodged in my throat. These religious leaders were creating a mob with their lies.

The leaders stayed where they were, boldly bragging to each other about their part in the plot to take Jesus. They rehearsed what they would do to make sure their plan worked.

I was an outsider to their schemes, but I felt guilty for not speaking against their lies. But who was I against all these? I leaned against the wall, wrapping my cloak more tightly around me, as if by its warmth, I would find an answer that would save Jesus. But I only grew colder as I realized there was nothing I could do to save Jesus from what they planned. I felt numb. Fear sliced at my heart. I felt numb. I remembered His request for prayer. Now I prayed, like I should have done before.

The faint light of dawn was on us when the soldiers returned Jesus to Pilate. Apparently news of the night's events had been spreading, because a crowd followed behind the soldiers, breaking the stillness of the dawn with their gossiping whispers. Their noise kept me from hearing the exchange between Pilate and the soldiers, but it seemed Herod had refused to sentence Jesus. In that, I felt relief.

But even as that feeling came, it was stomped out by the shouts of the leaders who clamored for his death.

Pilate argued with them, even offering to substitute Barabbas for Jesus.

More people had gathered, watching the battle of wills play out. Many hated the Jewish leaders, but all of them hated Rome.

One lone voice began. I couldn't hear what it said, only that it was repeated over and over. More took up the chant. When I finally understood the words, I gasped.

"Cru-ci-fy Him! Cru-ci-fy Him!"

There was a rhythm to the chant that indicated a riot.

Soldiers moved among the people, fearing an uprising.

My head swam. I leaned against a building for support. I held my head as if it could help me understand what was going on. My Lord would be crucified? What had He done?

I watched silently.

The chanting had taken on a life of its own. The entire crowd was echoing the words in unison.

What could I say?

I sank to the ground, holding my head, denying what they were doing to my Lord. How could this be happening?

When I finally looked up, the crowd had been silenced. But the damage had already been done. The sentence of death had been made.

Nothing could alter it.

The sun was rising over the hill as I gazed toward the top of the mountain, the Place of the Skull. The hill stood outside the city, away from the better section of town, for it was where criminals were crucified. Crucifixion was Rome's gruesome torture; a painful death meant for criminals. But today I would watch my Master be crucified.

The crowds followed the two criminals and Jesus up the hill. They pushed me along with them. I stumbled.

A Roman soldier hauled me to my feet. He wanted no cause for a riot.

But he couldn't stop the turmoil that churned inside me. My Lord was going to be crucified. And I could do nothing.

At the top of the mountain, I could see the entire city. Who could help now?

I couldn't watch as the soldiers drove the spikes into Jesus's hands and feet. But that didn't stop me from hearing each blow of the hammer against the spike, followed by His grunt of pain. I still hear that noise and cringe.

I risked a glance as the pounding stopped, only to see the soldiers raised the cross and dropped it into the hole, I turned my head, but still heard the thud as it hit bottom, jarring His body against the spikes before it settled into the ground.

I felt sick. The Passover meal had been the last thing I'd eaten, and it had churned all night. Now it left me.

Afterward, I wiped my mouth on the back of my hand.

I noticed Jesus's mother and a group of women gathered by the cross. Maybe joining them would help me. We needed to be together.

I hugged Mary. What words could I say to comfort?

The sun slowly moved across the sky. The hecklers jabbed and ridiculed, their words false and silly in light of the Man Who stayed on the cross.

I remembered the glory and God's voice at the top of that other mountain. "This is My Son in Whom I am well pleased."

I blinked, wiping my eyes. How could God be well pleased now?

Jesus had served us.

What greater servant could there be than One Who gave His life for me?

I had wanted so much to be the leader, the one who told others what to do. Isn't that what James and I always fought about—who would win this time? I had failed Jesus, just like Judas had betrayed Christ, and Peter had denied Christ. I had failed to serve. Because I wanted to lead. My God had told me to pray, so I wouldn't fall into temptation. I had failed, like everyone else.

I couldn't watch His suffering. Yet I couldn't leave. Every time I glanced up, I saw the blood seeping from His body, His strength leaving. I bowed my head and cried.

Mary was sobbing.

Her son James spoke, "Mother, I'll take you home."

She shook her head.

James seemed at a loss as to how to take away her pain. He glanced up at the cross and grimaced then looked away, as if Jesus had caused his mother's pain. He paced a few steps away from her; then returned. "Mother, I'm going home. I'll take you, if you wish."

She didn't respond.

He left.

She continued to weep.

I knelt down and put my arm around her, like Jesus would have done.

The two of us remained.

Jesus lifted himself up to grab a breath. "Woman," he gasped, "behold your son!"

Then, raising Himself again with great effort, He looked at me. "Behold, your mother."

Jesus's words had always been important, few and full of truth. But now, as He struggled for every breath, each word held great weight. By them, I felt forgiven. He didn't expect me to stop His death. Instead, He told me how to still serve Him. I held Mary and nodded. The love Jesus had shown, I would show to His mother. I would be there for her.

But as quickly as I had felt the relief of being able to do something for Jesus, it died.

I licked my dry lips, feeling only an aching numbness. What was the point of loving?

Jesus had loved perfectly, only to be killed by hate.

If the Son of God could not win against evil, who could?

We sat there in a huddle on the ground beneath the cross. Waiting. Waiting for the end that we did not want.

The sky drew dark. Thunder rolled, echoing across the mountains. I didn't notice until lighting blasted through the sky and hit close by, outlining the cross and the Man upon it. The storm, so fierce, shook the mountain.

I stayed there, holding Mary in my arms, as others ran from the mountain for shelter in the valley.

No danger could compare to the death of the Son of God.

I squeezed Mary tighter as I covered us both with my cloak. The rain poured from the sky, blending with my own tears. Water mingled with the blood that had pooled at the base of His cross and ran in torrents down the mountain.

I looked at the Man. He no longer breathed.

Instead of feeling relief that He no longer suffered, I felt a heaviness that couldn't be shaken. What should I do? I squeezed Mary; not that she felt anything. She looked as lost as I felt.

I helped her to her feet and led her to my house. I led her to my own bed and covered her with a sheepskin.

I paced outside my doorway. I couldn't sleep. Why couldn't I have stayed awake to pray when Jesus had asked? Now I had stayed up all night and day without thought of sleep.

I didn't think I could cry anymore. But I did.

Time seemed distorted. I felt people move around me, preparing meals, but I couldn't eat. Didn't they understand what had happened?

Could life continue when God was dead?

I wandered over to Peter's house. The other disciples were there. Andrew told me Judas had hung himself.

"Too late to do any good," I responded. Why couldn't he have hung himself before betraying our Lord? I might've felt sorry for him then. Even as the words were out of my mouth, I saw Jesus's look in my mind. He had forgiven me.

How could I forgive Judas?

We sat around, silent.

Even Peter stayed quiet. I glanced at him to remind myself that he was still in the room.

What should we do now?

On Sunday, I woke to pounding on my door. After pulling a cloak around myself, I opened the door. Mary Magdalene stood there, her eyes wide with anger and fright. "They've taken the Lord. The tomb is empty!"

I ran to get Peter, and together we went to see. Wasn't it bad enough for them to have killed Jesus, without stealing His body? Anger boiled through my blood. My legs propelled me ahead of Peter.

I didn't know what I would do once I got there. But when I arrived at the tomb, it was open. The Roman seal was broken. The guards were gone.

I stooped and looked in. It took several moments for my eyes to adjust to the darkness. Only the light from the rising sun illuminated the stone bench where his body had lain. I squinted to see better in the dim light. Something wasn't right, but I couldn't tell what it was from this distance. What had they done with Him?

Peter arrived then. He didn't stop at the door but ran inside, calling back to me, "They better not have taken Him!"

I followed him inside. "If they have, I'll . . ." What could I do? I hadn't stopped His death. I couldn't stop what they did now . . . . I looked around me, unable to say more.

The wrappings of death still lay as if His body had been sucked from them. His face-cloth was rolled up separately. I touched it lightly, remembering how He had looked as He took His last breath.

Peter brought me back to the present, muttering, "They couldn't have taken Him."

I had no answer to that.

I circled the bench that had held His body. It didn't hold the sorrow it had held before, because His body wasn't there.

Still, I didn't understand.

Later, when Jesus appeared to us in His resurrected body, He explained more. Things began to make sense.

This time I paid more attention.

Then Jesus left for heaven and the Holy Spirit came upon me. He reminded me, almost like James always had, whenever I was tempted to do wrong. Only the Lord's Spirit nudged me *before* I did it. He impressed me with the truth of Jesus's message, the truth that would set people free.

The Spirit prompted me to write, to tell others about Jesus as the Son of God. Matthew and Mark had already written about Jesus. But I focused on how Jesus was the Son of God. Who better to witness of what He had done than me?

I closed my account by saying, "Jesus did many other signs besides these, but these are written so you may believe Jesus is the Christ, the Son of God; so that when you believe you may have life in His Name." What more is needed?

Peter and I became a team. He'd do the talking, and I would serve the people behind the scenes. That didn't mean I never talked, nor that I didn't struggle sometimes with serving, but the Lord was helping me learn to show His love.

Sometimes I felt Jesus was right there. I'd turn to lean on Him, and He wouldn't be there. Peter would sense my longing and pat his chest. "He's right here, John. He hasn't left us."

I'd nod and smile.

It wasn't the same, but it was.

We were going to the Temple to preach when a lame beggar shook his cup of coins. "Just a shekel, if you please."

Peter said, "I don't have any silver and gold. But I'll give you what I do have. In the Name of Jesus Christ of Nazareth, get up and walk."

The beggar stood and praised God. He worshipped and danced.

I grabbed his arms and danced with him.

The truth of God's message was still here with us!

Next thing I knew, we were being thrown into prison, just because we told others about Jesus's resurrection.

Peter preached to the rulers who held us.

They counseled together, not knowing what to do with us. Finally, they let us go with a warning. "Don't speak about Jesus again."

I answered, "Whether it's right to obey you, rather than God, you be the judge; for we can't stop speaking about what we know is true."

They threatened us, but let us go, mostly on account of the people.

The people were thirsty to hear, like the woman at the well, but the rulers wanted to control, like Judas, who refused to see truth.

I learned in those years, not only the love of my Lord, but how to love and serve others. His Holy Spirit would nudge me into acts that I normally wouldn't do and encourage me to say things that would let others know the truth, regardless of the suffering that would come to me.

As I grew older, the love of the Lord was so intertwined with His truth, I couldn't separate them. If I couldn't tell others His truth, then I wasn't showing them His love.

Doesn't truth give freedom?

Those false teachers were quick to tell me I wasn't loving to them. Of course not! They were deceiving people. I called them wolves in sheep's clothes! Vipers! Worthy of damnation!

Didn't Jesus call the religious leaders "white-washed tombs"? I felt anger rise within me toward those deceivers who convinced others of their lies.

Love was found in truth.

Some said I was too harsh. What happened to the love that I preached? Love without truth isn't love: its control.

I had been the youngest disciple of Jesus. I had found a sense of pride in that position. But as the other disciples were tortured and killed, some with excruciating suffering, I wondered why I lingered. What did the Lord have for me?

I thought my end had come when I was put in boiling oil to make me recant my beliefs. The oil warmed me, that is true. But it caused me no harm.

I think my tormentors gave up on me. Soon afterward, they sent me to Patmos, an island desolate of most everything. I was to remain there until my death. I guess they thought I could do no harm there.

But God . . .

I laughed. But God always works in ways we can't expect. He gave me a vision of His Second Coming. I had written about His First Coming and shown He was the Son of God. He came to seek and to save those who were lost. We expected Him to come as King, but He came as servant.

His Second Coming? . . . Wow! He would come as Judge of all, as King of kings, as Victor to claim His people, His possessions, and all His earth. Nothing would stop Him.

I had doubted at His death why evil seemed to triumph over good. By His resurrection, He had conquered death and sin. But we were still living in this world, full of evil.

With the Second Coming, suffering will stop. Evil will be conquered. All those leaders who insisted on working evil will be judged.

Such victory!

I've mellowed over the years. I still get angry, especially over false teachers. Read my letters to the churches.

But my Jesus has been gracious to give me His love, teach me His truth, and fill me with His peace that all things will work out as He deemed right.

Expectations?

How can I expect anything but good from the Hands of my Jesus, Who loves, Who is truth, and Who is just?

Expectations

Who did the Jews expect Jesus to be?

They expected Him to come in glory. He was placed in a manger by a lowly virgin.

They expected a king. He came to serve.

They expected Him to overthrow Rome. He came as an obedient subject.

They expected His subjects to be educated. They were unlearned fishermen that were to become like children.

They expected paid positions. He asked for their hearts.

They expected the Jews' Messiah. He touched a Samaritan woman, and healed a Roman centurion's servant. He came for the entire world.

They expected condemnation of publicans, sinners and prostitutes. He forgave, inviting them to follow Him.

They gloried in self-reliance. He told his disciples, "Not My will, but My Father's."

They thought they knew the way of righteousness. He said, "I am the only Way."

When betrayed, He expected it.

When beaten, He took it.

When rejected, He stood alone.

They didn't surprise Him; they fulfilled His plans.

They didn't take his life, He gave it.

His actions surprised them.

His words silenced them.

His life rebuked them.

No one expected His resurrection.

No one expected His victory over sin, death, and the grave.

No one expected that He would have the last Word. Until He did.

What do you expect of Jesus?

Put your expectations aside.

See Jesus through the eyes of those who met Him.

Then know Him by the truth He reveals.

About the Author

Expecting God's blessing on her marriage to her best friend as they seek to follow God, Sonya Contreras hasn't been disappointed.

Expecting God to do great things isn't always easy in the midst of diapers, laundry, and the dirt of raising eight boys in the foothills of the Sequoia Mountains, but Sonya has found God's faithfulness surpasses all her expectations.

Expecting God's leading as she writes can only bring His nod of approval. That is her desire.

She writes about what matters at www.sonyacontreras.com.

About the Illustrator

Lois Rosio Sprague is a native of Glen Ellyn, Illinois. She studied at the American Academy of Art in Chicago, under the direction of Irving Shapiro. There she received two degrees, one in fine art, the other in graphic art.

Relocating to the mountains of Colorado, Lois's work includes large scale portraits and murals. She has gained a reputation for her portraiture, which makes her warm, sensitive approach and bold, colorful style increasingly sought after. She successfully portrays people from all walks of life, cultures, and ages.

Lois has been highlighted in numerous exhibits and galleries, and has been showcased at National Conventions Performing Live Art. Her diverse talents include children's book illustration, commissioned portraits and murals.

Lois has a deep attachment to the outdoors. She is most passionate about painting people. She is a committed Christian and strives to share the glory and grace of God in her work. Lois and her husband Gary have five grown children, which give her many reasons for capturing genuine human emotion through her paintings.

Her works are displayed at www.loisrosiosprague.com/illustration

Other Books
by Sonya Contreras

Tell of My Kingdom's Glory Series tells the love story between God and His people.

In **Book One:** *Until My Name Is Known,* God brings His people to see Him as He frees them from the bonds of Egypt.

In **Book Two:** *I Have Called You by Name,* God draws His people to know Him, as He provides safety through the demands of His Law and teaches dependence upon Him to reach their Land.

In **Book Three:** *I Am with You,* God reassures His people that, as He had been with Moses, so would He be with them. He brings them into the Land promised them, giving rest from their journey.

Our Story of His Lessons: Twenty Years of Christmas News

People ask about our boys and how we do it. The yearly letters found here give you a glimpse into those answers.

We've lived in the foothills of the Sequoias for over eighteen years. Almost half of the boys were born in the house. We've set down roots, not only in our garden and with our animals but in our hearts where the land has helped us settle. We share memories on a yearly basis of what God teaches us, thus the chronicles of the Christmas letters.

Let Her Hear: Parables from a Mom

These parables (devotionals) are not a substitute for careful, study of the Word. They give a starting point to focus on where God wants you to be all day, a help to see Him even while doing the mundane, routine, necessary, "mom" things in life. They remind you of the heavenly realm that's part of the earthly walk.

They were taken from articles previously written for my website and made into book form.

How Suffering Shows God's Love: A Paradox Explained

Pain opens the heart to search for meaning. We ask God, "Why?" and find He is silent. We question His goodness, love, and sovereignty. These questions bring us to Him.

By coming to Him, we learn the deeper answers. We find the love we crave. We discover the God Who wants us to know Him.

This collection of articles leads us to find that meaning, learn those answers, and see our God.

A current listing of books with summaries and excerpts can be found at www.sonyacontreras.com.

www.ingramcontent.com/pod-product-compliance
Lightning Source LLC
Chambersburg PA
CBHW080736250626
47170CB00010B/2848